I

Kelly McWinter P.I. Book 3

by

Jude Pittman

PUBLISHED BY:

Books We Love Ltd.
Chestermere, Alberta
Canada

ISBN: 978-1-927476-86-4

Copyright 2012 by Jude Pittman
Cover art by 2012 Michelle Lee

Dedication

To my brother Ken Sullivan, who has applauded and encouraged every one of my books, and is always the first customer in line

~~~

Chapter One

"Hang onto your hat," Kelly McWinter warned as he spun the steering wheel and herded his rented Jeep Cherokee into a sharp right turn. Off the highway the road narrowed into two lanes and dropped straight down to the ocean.

"Breathtaking." Gillian Tanner, a striking blond with bright blue eyes and sun-kissed skin, pressed her nose against the windshield and laughed with pleasure as they made the heart-stopping descent.

Texans to the core, Kelly and Gillian were visiting the Oregon fishing resort of Bubba Tate, a longtime friend from their home in Indian Creek, Texas.

"I think that's Paradise Lodge." Kelly pointed towards a cluster of buildings spread along a ledge overlooking the ocean. Minutes later he pulled off the road in front of a log building that gleamed red gold in the afternoon sunlight.

Kelly had no sooner stopped the Jeep than Bubba, hopping and leaping on his game leg, yanked open the door and grabbed Kelly's arm pumping it for all he was worth.

"Hot damn. I've about stomped down the deck waitin' for y'all to git here."

"This is some spread." Kelly extricated himself from the little guy's clutches and circled the Jeep to open Gillian's door.

"Yep, it's a dandy." Bubba unlatched the back

and grabbed suitcases. "I've got you two set up in the most secluded cabin on the place." He handed a bag to Kelly and grabbed the next one. "I'll take you down so you can get the trail dust off. But I'll expect you back at the lodge in a heartbeat. I've so much to tell you it'll take days to shut me down."

"It's a deal." Kelly slapped his friend on the back and grabbed another case. "Let's get this stuff to the cabin. Gilly and I will freshen up and then I'm all ears."

At the cabin they'd been working in silence for several minutes, unpacking cases and setting out toiletries, when Gillian turned from the suitcase she'd been unpacking and slanted her eyes in Kelly's direction. "That was some view I had coming up from the lodge."

"Yeah." Kelly, said from where he was bent the suitcase with a handful of socks in his hand. "Those big cedars are pretty awesome."

"Actually I was referring to the backside of the long tall Texan I was following up the path. Of course those trees were gorgeous too. Kind of like sentries guarding the ocean. But it's hard to concentrate on the landscape when your eyes are focused on tight butt muscles."

Kelly lifted his head and fixed his slate blue eyes on Gillian's baby blues. The socks, forgotten in his hands, tumbled into the suitcase.

"Sounds like somebody wants to play. He closed the distance between them in two strides and swept Gillian into his arms. "I wonder how long it'll take Bubba to come banging on that door."

"Guess we're going to find out," Gillian wrapped her arms around Kelly's neck and murmured into his ear.

Kelly unbuttoned his shirt, dropped his jeans and stepped out of his jockeys, all the while leading Gillian across the room towards the bed.

"Wait," she said, pulling her t-shirt over her head, wriggling her shorts and panties down her legs and kicking them off her feet.

"Can't wait," Kelly said, wrapping his arms around her waist and falling backwards onto the bed.

Gillian moaned when he gripped her nipples between his fingers and rubbed. His mouth found hers and she surrendered her tongue. Drawing her in, Kelly plundered, sucking her tongue and licking her lips while his fingers kneaded her nipples.

"Oh my God," Gillian wrapped her arms around his neck and rolled with him as he flipped her over and came down on top with his legs between hers and his manhood hard and ready. Spreading for him, she rose to meet him, opening herself and inviting him inside.

They came together skin slapping skin, both of them giving and taking, until a thundering climax drove them over the edge and into blissful oblivion.

"Don't expect me to move for at least an hour," Gillian warned.

"Oh no you don't. I'd say if we aren't showered and out of here in the next ten minutes, Bubba's cane will be banging hell out of that door."

Gillian groaned and pulled the pillow over her head.

* * *

A half hour later, sporting freshly-showered glows, Kelly and Gillian joined Bubba in the Lodge's living room.

"I was about to send out the dogs," Bubba grumbled. His mile-wide smile let them know he understood the delay.

Kelly's gaze traveled around the trophy-laden room. Leather couches stood in front of a stone fireplace. Across the room, a wall of windows looking straight out to the ocean served as an awesome backdrop for the long leather bar that sparkled with crystal.

"This is some setup," he said, turning to Bubba and spreading his arms to indicate the room around them.

"You ain't seen nothing. Come on over here." Bubba led them through an archway into an open-beamed lounge where a giant screen TV flashed images of a football game in progress. Tables and chairs cozily circled the gigantic dance floor on one side of the room and four regulation sized pool tables dominated the other side. "It's a bit roomier than the bait-house," Bubba drawled.

All three of them shared a chuckle at the memory of the tin and tarpaper shack that had been Bubba's home-away-from-home at Indian Creek until Anna Davis' legacy left him rich enough to realize his dreams and buy the fishing resort in Oregon.

"What time do you expect Stella and Cam?" Gillian asked.

Stella was the bride half of the reason Kelly and Gillian had made the trip to Paradise Lodge. A year ago she'd hired Kelly, who had his Texas PI license, to clear her niece Mikki from a murder charge.

During the course of the investigation Kelly had introduced Stella to his best friend Cam Belscher, proud owner of Indian Creek's Hideaway Bar & Barbecue, and by the time Kelly solved the murder, Stella and Cam were engaged. They made the announcement the night everyone got together at the Hideaway to celebrate Mikki's freedom, and Bubba volunteered to host the wedding at his newly acquired Lodge in Oregon.

"That's one damn determined woman." Bubba said, shoving his cowboy hat back on his head and swiping his arm across his forehead. "She's been chewing the bit all week to get down here and see to things, but I made Cam promise to keep her outta my hair until tomorrow."

"Smart thinking." Kelly and Gillian spoke in unison.

Refreshments, consisting of heaping plates of super crispy Nachos and frosty longnecks, brought to the table by a couple of snappy young waiters.

Kelly's eyes widened at the sight. "Guess this grub proves the old saying `You can take the boy out of Texas, but you can't take Texas out of the boy.'"

The three friends spent the next few hours catching up on news from home and reminiscing about the old days. By the time conversation slowed, the afternoon sun had dipped deep into the horizon. "Look at the sunset," Gillian called from where she'd strolled out onto the balcony. "No wonder you fell in love with this place."

* * *

Saturday morning a light breeze danced the bedroom curtains and glints of sunlight showed promise of an ideal day for the wedding.

"I'm going to find Stella and see if I can give her a hand." Gillian set a cup of coffee on the bedside table and bent for a morning kiss.

"Coffee. Thanks, but I had other ideas for the morning."

"I'll bet you did." Gillian laughed and backed a safe step away from the bed. "Bubba's having a buffet breakfast in the main lounge. You might want to move your buns out of bed and over there before he gets a notion to give you a personal wakeup call."

"Yeah. You're probably right. Can't take the bait man outta the country boy no matter how many fancy houses he's got. He gets up with the fish and doesn't see any reason the rest of us shouldn't be on the same schedule."

"See you later." Gillian stepped outside and pulled the door shut. Skirting the main lodge, she followed the ridge line up a steep path that led to a large cabin perched on the tip of a high rock ledge and offering a 180° view of the ocean below.

Gillian followed the path up to a flight of steps carved out of the rock. At the top, she stepped onto a wrap-around balcony. Some digs she observed as she stopped in front of a polished oak door and lifted the heavy brass knocker.

"It's open." Stella's muffled voice came through the door.

Gillian stepped inside and caught her breath.

Wow. She gasped out loud.

The west wall consisted of a solid sheet of glass that gave the illusion the room was suspended in clouds. A sandstone fireplace glinted with specks of gold. Sunbeams played with crystal prisms dangling from a chandelier and spreading a rainbow of colors across the white leather sofa.

"A girl could get used to this kind of living." Stella padded into the room, wrapped in a thick terry robe, her bright red hair caught in a matching towel.

"You are absolutely glowing." Gillian gave her friend in an exuberant hug. "This is breathtaking. Are you excited?"

"That would be an understatement." Stella parked herself on the corner of the sofa and pulled the towel off of her hair. "I had to pinch myself when I woke up this morning. Can you believe it? Me, getting married again, and to a true blue homegrown Texas cowboy."

Gillian gave Stella a once over and chuckled. "I bet that glow you're sporting has a lot more to do with your bed mate than this amazing cabin you slept in last night."

"Shhh, Bubba assigned us separate cabins until after the wedding."

Gillian laughed all the harder. "Silly man if he thought that was going to keep you apart. So tell me, what do you need me to do? This is the first time I've been anyone's maid of honor. I'm not sure I know all the protocol."

"The only thing I need you to do is keep me

company and help me handle the butterflies dancing around in my tummy."

"Got that. How about I get us some coffee?"

"In the pot on the counter. Two sugar, no cream. I'll finish putting my face on and join you in a minute."

Gillian poured two mugs of coffee, slid open one of the glass panels and stepped out into the clouds. Looking down, she swallowed a couple of times to get her stomach out of her throat. Breathtaking. The same glass that made up the walls in the living room also formed the floor on this side of the patio. Gingerly she approached a wrought iron table, set their mugs on the glass top and bent her head to look down. As far as her eye could see shrub covered cliffs dropped thousands of feet into the churning waters below.

"Sure is some sight for a Texas country girl." She said when Stella joined her at the table.

"I'll say. I've stayed in some mansions in my time, but this beats anything I've ever seen. That Bubba sure knows how to put on the dog."

The women shared a laugh and spent the next hour catching up on who was doing what to whom and why in the close knit community of Indian Creek.

"It's amazing how quickly River Oaks has faded off my radar and how much like home the Hideaway has become." Stella took a sip of coffee and smiled over the rim.

"Tell me about it." Gillian agreed. "I had no idea what was about to happen to me when I accepted that barbecue invitation last summer."

"Sounds like I'm not the only one bitten by the Indian Creek cupid." Stella's laughter echoed into the open spaces and a couple of red spots appeared on Gillian's cheeks.

"I didn't realize it was that obvious." She lowered her eyes and lifted her cup to her lips.

"Hey. Don't worry. We're sisters in here." Stella pointed to her heart. "I know exactly how you feel."

The two women chatted amiably while they finished their coffee. Finally, Stella pushed her cup aside. "Guess we'd better get this done." She rose and invited Gillian to follow her into the bedroom.

"I feel a bit silly doing the white bridal routine, but it's the first time around for Cam and it only seemed fair."

"This dress is gorgeous." Gillian lifted the yards of satin and slipped the gleaming white dress over Stella's head.

"You think?"

"I know. My God, you're a vision. Come over here, look in the mirror."

Together they crossed to a full length mirror and Stella caught her breath. "Is that me? Wow, guess I know what they mean about the dress making the woman."

"No way. It's the woman making the dress this time around."

* * *

Standing in front of an altar formed out of thick pines bowed and crossed overhead, rays of light streamed through the trees as the sun beamed its blessing on Cam and Stella. The bride, stunning in her white sheath with fingertip veil tilted her head and looked into the groom's deep brown eyes.

Pride lit up Cam's face and he smiled down at his bride. Decked out in a sharp new western tux with a crisp white shirt. His jet black hair had been styled to keep that one particular lock from flopping into his eyes, and he looked for all the world like a romance novel cover model.

"You're the most beautiful woman in the world." He whispered.

"Well, maybe this corner of Oregon right at the moment. You clean up pretty damn smart yourself," she quipped. They laughed together and stole a quick kiss, before the rising notes of the organ brought them back to the present and they turned their attention to the ceremony.

* * *

"What an absolutely perfect wedding." Gillian's eyes sparkled as she sat on the side of the bed and began to undress. "And the food. I'm so full I may never get up again."

"Great for the waistline. Kelly chuckled and patted his midriff.

"Wasn't Stella gorgeous? They both looked so happy."

"Yep. They're a darn good fit, those two."

Sleep came fast. It seemed like minutes later Kelly woke to sound of banging on the cabin door.

"Hang on." He sprang out of bed, grabbed his

pants and stumbled across the room.

"What the heck." He muttered, as he fumbled with the latch and yanked on the door.

"Sorry." Bubba stood outside with a flashlight aimed at the door. "Old Rob from Gillian's stable just called. They found Larry Preston's body in one of her stalls."

"Shit." Kelly pulled the door closed and stepped out on the porch with Bubba.

"Larry Preston? Are you sure. He's just a kid."

"That's what I said to Rob. And yeah, he's sure. He knows the Preston brothers. There's three of them and Larry's the youngest. There's going to be hell to pay that's for sure."

"I better tell Gillian. She'll want to call Rob."

"I'll get some coffee brewing."

"Thanks."

"What's wrong?" Gillian poked her head out the doorway and blinked in the light from Bubba's flash.

"Let's go inside." Kelly put his arm around her shoulder, nodded at Bubba and led Gillian back inside the cabin.

"There's been some trouble at the stable." Kelly tightened his grip.

"What?" She pulled back, her eyes searching his face trying to read his expression.

"Larry Preston has been found dead inside the stables. Nobody knows what happened."

"Oh my God. I've got to get home." As the owner of the Lake Country Riding Academy, Gillian employed a fulltime groom and one other instructor besides herself. The rest of the staff were students who worked part-time.

"I know. You pack, I'll arrange our flights."

Kelly got busy on the phone while Gillian filled her suitcase.

"I've got us on a 9:30 flight to Fort Worth," Kelly said when Gillian, who had been on her cell with her young assistant, hung up and joined him at the bed where he was taking care of his own packing.

"How's Angelina holding up?" Kelly closed his case and set it on the floor beside Gillian's.

"She sounded so scared. She's trying hard to be brave, but she's only seventeen. It's bad enough reading about murder but when it happens to someone you know it's devastating."

"It's tough on all of you. But if it's humanly possible we'll be on that flight. Meanwhile, Rob's got a good head on his shoulders. He'll see that the kids are okay until we get back. Besides, I'm sure their parents have rallied round. They know you're out of town."

"I'm worried about the horses too. They're bound to be spooked. Quarter horses are extremely sensitive."

"I know. The sooner we get on the road the better." Kelly picked up their cases and the two of them headed for the lodge, where Bubba met them with hot coffee and pastries packed for their trip.

"It's a couple hours drive, you'll need something." He placed the containers on the dash and turned to give them both a hug.

"Be safe." Bubba said after they'd climbed into the Jeep.

"Thanks Bubba. I'll call you when we get things

settled." Kelly headed down the road.

"Do you think we'll make it in time?" Gillian asked.

"It'll be close. But we're going to try. Don't worry. We'll get back as quick as we can."

Chapter Two

Augustus Graham, a large black man known to his friends as Gus, filled the doorway of Gillian's ranch style kitchen. "Hey Kelly. Good to see you. Sorry it has to be under these circumstances."

"Thanks Gus. I guess the only bright spot in this mess is the fact that you're in charge of the investigation."

"How's Gillian holding out?"

"She's keeping it together, but it's rough. These kids are like family. Right now she's out in the stables settling down the horses." Kelly motioned towards the kitchen table. "Grab a seat. If you've time for a cup I'll put the coffee on and maybe you can bring me up to date."

"Sounds good. I could use a cuppa Bubba's special about now." The two of them shared a laugh at the memory of the molasses-like brew Bubba used to serve down at the Indian Creek bait house. "How's the little guy doing? The creek don't seem the same without him."

"He's great. If you get out of the concrete jungle long enough to take a vacation you've got to take Betty to his place in Oregon. It'd do you both good."

"Now don't you get started." Gus rolled his eyes. "I'm already in hot water with Betty over the number of vacation days I've got banked."

Kelly set a cup in front of Gus. "Same old Gus." He poured them each a cup and put the pot within easy reach. "So what do you know about this Preston kid?"

"He's the youngest of four. The old man's a boozer. We've had him in and out of the drunk tank for years. Mom's okay. One of those long suffering women who's got a blind spot when it comes to any of her men folk."

"I know the type. What about the kid?"

Gus shook his head. "About what you'd figure. Drugs, booze, the usual wild parties and a couple of short spells in Juvie."

"Gangs?"

"Not to my knowledge. Of course we've had no reason to check. Now we'll get into everything--associates, activities, and habits. There's got to be a reason why an eighteen year old kid is hit over the head with enough force to scramble his brains."

"He was killed by a blow to the head?"

"That's right. With something smooth and very hard--maybe a shovel, or some kind of farm implement. We're still looking."

"I suppose there's no chance he simply fell and hit his head."

Gus squinted at Kelly and scowled.

"Okay." Kelly held up his hands. "I guess I'm spending too much time in the company of civilians."

"To answer that, not that it warrants an answer. There's not a chance in hell this death is anything other than cold blooded murder."

"Yeah." Kelly sighed. "Poor Gilly's in for a rough time."

"You want to give us a hand?"

"I'd like to. If you don't have any objection."

Gus chuckled. "Helluva lot of good it would do me if I did. But no. Matter of fact, I'll be glad of the help."

"Hi Gus." Gillian said from the doorway. "It's nice to see you again. Although I wish the reason was different."

"Me too. I'm sorry about your loss. Were you close to the lad?"

"No, not especially. He wasn't one of my regulars--just an extra who helped out in the stables during the summer. But it doesn't matter. He still shouldn't have been murdered."

"Do you feel up to giving me a rundown on the stables? Just an overview for now, like how many kids work here, their names and if you've had concerns about any of them, that kind of stuff."

"I'll get you a coffee." Kelly pulled out a chair and motioned for Gillian to sit while he got her a cup and poured.

"Thanks." She smiled up at Kelly and then turned her attention back to Gus. "I have five regular kids. They alternate every other day after school and one weekend day. There's Angelina Morales. She's what you might call my administrative assistant. She's a senior in high school. Then there are the four boys. I have Mike Armstrong and Kevin Cummings working Monday, Wednesday and Friday and Paul King and Toby Martin working Tuesday, Thursday and Sunday. The other two, Larry Preston and Robin Barlow, are casuals. They work alternate Saturdays, which is a light day--just feed and a basic muck out and we call one or both them in whenever we need extra help."

"I think I've met Angelina. She's the attractive brunette with the big brown eyes that are sure to break a lot of hearts."

Gillian laughed. "That's Angelina. She is beautiful. Except she's the type of girl that will probably be on the receiving end of any heartbreaking that's done. Everyone loves her. She's a sweetheart and I'm certain she isn't involved with Larry. He's a good looking guy--or rather he was--but he's kind of wild. Not Angelina's type."

"You'd be surprised how many girls like Angelina fall for wild boys." Gus turned to Kelly who nodded agreement.

"I don't know her that well," Kelly said, "but my take is that if she knows anything about Larry's murder, she'll tell Gillian first chance she gets."

Gillian nodded. "Yes. I'm sure of that too. It's been crazy since we got home so I haven't had a chance to talk to the kids about anything other than the horses. I will though and if any of them knows anything, I'm sure they'll tell me."

"Sounds fair." Gus turned to Kelly. "How would you like to come on board for this investigation?"

"You mean officially?"

"Yep. The Commissioner's approved an investigator position a few months ago. I've been waiting for the right man to fill the spot—matter of fact I'd planned on giving you a call to see if there might be any interest."

"Wow. You've kind of caught me flatfooted. I'd

rather work with you than anyone on earth. I just hadn't really planned on going official again."

"I know." Gus chuckled. "But I figured this investigation might be a good time for you to try us on for size."

"You old dog." Kelly laughed. "What if it doesn't fit?"

"No problem. The job's semi-permanent, if it works great if not, you go back to doing your own thing."

"Couldn't say fairer than that. Might work to our advantage too. The kids know I'm a former cop, but they also know I'm Gillian's friend. They'll be more inclined to trust me than a stranger. I'll wander out to the stables after a bit and talk to the boys. That okay with you?" He turned to Gillian for confirmation.

"Fine with me. Toby and Paul are there now. Do you want me to get Angelina to join us?" She turned back to Gus.

"Maybe later. First I'd like you to give me a rundown on the stables. What do those kids do besides cleaning the barns? Any chance they're involved in some kind of bookmaking scheme? You know horses and gambling kind of go together."

Gillian laughed. "Gus. You city boy. That's thoroughbred racing. I raise quarter horses. They're racers too, but it's different. Mainly they're show horses and rodeo competitors. They don't run the kind of races that attract big time gamblers."

"Oh." Gus grinned. "So what do you raise them for?"

"The American Quarter horse is the best riding

horse in the world. They're used for all kinds of things: show horse, race horse, reining and cutting horse, rodeo competitor, ranch horse. I could go on and on."

"Okay." Gus chuckled. "I get the idea. What about drugs? Any indication of that kind of activity?"

"My God I hope not." Gillian ran her hands down her face. "I guess anything's possible nowadays. But I'd be sick if I thought one of my kids was involved with drugs."

"We'll check them out. Can you think of anything that's happened around here that has seemed out of the ordinary?"

"That's just it, I can't. I've been thinking back over everything we've been doing for the past two months and there's nothing. I don't really have what you would call a personal relationship with the kids, except Angelina, of course. But I am friendly with them. Before this happened I would have sworn that I knew them well enough to recognize anything serious enough to lead to murder. Is it possible that Larry could have been mistaken for someone else? What about his brothers? I don't know them, but I've heard stories about those boys and drug activity. Wasn't one of them just released from jail?"

"That would be Clinton," Gus replied. "We've already considered the possibility of Larry's brother's being involved--or even that this was some kind of retaliation killing for something involving one of Larry's brothers. We'll be investigating those possibilities. We're going to cover all angles, that's why we need to do a thorough check on his friends and co-workers, to eliminate them.

Gillian nodded understanding and turned a wan smile to Kelly. "If you and Gus will excuse me, I need to change out of my traveling clothes."

"You should lay down for awhile." Kelly slipped his arm around her shoulder. "You didn't get more than two hours sleep last night. Gus, do you need anything that won't keep?"

Gus shook his head. "We're good for now. You go take care of yourself. I'll have a chat with Kelly and then be on my way back to the station."

"Do you want to take a walk out back?" Kelly asked.

Gus nodded. "Good idea."

Outside the two men strolled across the lawn and let themselves out the gate that led to the stables.

"This is probably going to be rough on Gillian," Gus said. "My gut tells me that we are going to find drugs--or something even nastier--at the bottom of this. And worse yet, from Gillian's point of view, is the sinking feeling I have that one or more of her regulars is going to be involved in this mess."

"I know. I've had that same bad feeling ever since we got here. What's more I don't think Angelina's telling us everything she knows. Maybe I'm oversensitive because of Gillian's position but something doesn't feel right."

"Nope. You're not oversensitive. I had exactly the same feeling. Do you want to have a go at her, or do you want me to haul her into town and shake her up a bit?"

They'd reached the stables and Kelly paused with his hand on the latch. "I'd consider having you do that if it wasn't for Gillian. But if you're willing to let me give it a go, how about I ask her some pointed questions and at the same time explain a few facts about withholding information from the police. I don't think Angelina's involved in drugs or anything like that. More likely she's protecting someone. But all those years undercover for DEA taught me to take nothing for granted. I'll approach her like I would any other suspect."

The two men stopped at the corral surrounding the barn and Gus planted his foot on one of the wooden rails.

"This isn't going to bring up too many bad memories, is it?"

Kelly winced at Gus' question, but they both knew his reference to the murder of Kelly's wife by a drug gang was appropriate. Lynda died because of Kelly's undercover drug work, and the similarities between that case and where this one might be leading were too obvious to overlook.

"I know where you're heading." Kelly said. "And I appreciate the concern. But this is an entirely different situation. Lynda was killed because of my work. She wasn't involved in the situation that led to her murder. Gillian, on the other hand, owns this place. Whatever is going on or has gone on is directly her concern. The fact that I am or am not involved will not increase her danger, and it just might, or at least I'd like to think it might, make things easier."

"Good. That's my take as well. Of course this may not have anything at all to do with drugs. But, considering that both of our instincts already have us looking in that direction, I thought it best to clear the air before we started. "Gus gripped Kelly's shoulder in a gesture of reassurance. "I'll head on back to town now. Give me a call if anything comes up, if not let's meet over at the White Bull for breakfast. Eight o'clock suit you?"

"Sounds great. I'm going to go down to the stables and nose around. Maybe I'll have a chat with whoever is working this weekend."

Gus left and Kelly went to the barn. Inside he walked along the aisle past horse stalls whose occupants were out to pasture for the day. Whispered voices traveled on a gust of wind and Kelly's cop sense went on high alert. Stepping into an empty stall he flattened himself against the wall.

"Are you sure the cops have gone?" The voice shook and Kelly strained to catch the frightened whispers.

"Yes. There's no one here but Kelly and Gillian, and they're inside." Kelly recognized Angelina's voice.

"What did you tell them?" The male tone--insistent and scared--echoed in the silent barn.

"I haven't talked to them yet. I've avoided everyone. But I'm not going to lie to Gillian. So you better find Sam and tell him that we're going to tell the truth and if he has any brains at all he'll go to the cops and tell them everything."

"You can't do that. We promised."

"No, you promised. I only agreed to let you talk to Sam before I said anything. I am not going to lie to Gillian. Now get out of here. Go tell Sam that he has until morning to tell the police what he knows or I'm telling Gillian everything."

Angelina's statement was followed by quick footsteps and the bang of the door. Kelly remained silent and waited. Moments later another door closed and Kelly stepped out into the aisle.

Kelly pondered the conversation and wondered which one of the boys had been in there with Angelina. He could, of course, go straight to Angelina and demand an explanation. But she'd already stated her intention of going to Gillian. He needed to pull back and let her make the call.

* * *

Later, after Gillian had finished stable rounds and said goodnight to the boys, Kelly uncorked a bottle of Merlot.

"Let's take these out to the swing." He handed her a glass and nodded towards the back door.

"Thanks." Gillian tucked her arm in his. "It seems like a dream, or should I say nightmare."

"I'm sure it does. I've been feeling a bit disoriented myself. Last night we were kicking up our heels at the wedding. Now here we are back home in the middle of God knows what kind of mess."

"Do you really think one of those kids is involved in Larry's death?"

They'd strolled along the porch to the long wooden swing where Gillian loved to curl up and read. Together they sat and snuggled close with Gillian tucked securely against Kelly's arm.

"I'm afraid there isn't much doubt." Kelly related the conversation he'd overheard between Angelina and the boy in the stable.

"Which one of the boys was she talking to?"

"I couldn't tell. He was hidden from my line of sight. Angelina was facing the door of my hiding place and I didn't dare move or she'd have spotted me. I had to wait until she left, and by the time I got over to where they'd been talking the boy had disappeared."

"That's too bad. Still it had to be either Paul or Toby."

"Not necessarily. One of the others might have stopped by because of the murder."

Gillian leaned into Kelly and kissed him hard. "Thank you for waiting to talk to me before approaching Angelina. I know it must have gone against your instincts and I appreciate that."

Kelly smiled and snuggled her closer to his chest. "It's your place, you've got the right to decide."

"In that case. I've decided it's time we had some dinner. You'll stay tonight won't you?"

"Sure. As long as you need me. I'm still on holidays so my time's my own. I'll just run by the Hideaway after dinner and see how Darlene's getting along with Jake. "

"Great. I'll go over to Angelina's and have a chat with her while you're gone. She'll probably be more at ease if I see her alone."

"Sounds like a plan. Want me to drop you off?"

"No you go ahead. There's no telling how long this is going to take. I'll just meet you back here later."

After a quick and tasty meal of fajitas and Caesar

salad Gillian left for Angelina's and Kelly got into Old Blue and headed for Indian Creek.

* * *

Seven years ago Kelly had been an undercover police officer, married to the love of his life and living a typical cop's life in Fort Worth. All that had ended when the bikers had been tipped off to Kelly's identity -- by a person or persons unknown -- and they'd retaliated by throwing a Molotov cocktail through the bedroom window of Kelly's apartment. There shouldn't have been anyone home.

Both Kelly and Lynda worked the night shift -- Lynda an ER nurse at the hospital and socializing with the Fort Worth's criminal element.

That particular night, they'd both had the night off. They'd been invited to the home of Kelly's mentor, Jim Forbes. His wife had planned a big surprise party to celebrate Jim's retirement. Both Kelly and Lynda were going, but a couple of hours before it was time to leave, Lynda had been struck with one of her migraines. She didn't get them often, but when she did the only thing that helped was a double-dose of the knock out medicine her doctor had prescribed for those occasions. Kelly had been torn between staying home with his sick wife and paying tribute to his mentor, but Lynda had insisted he attend the party. She'd already taken the pain medicine and by the time Kelly helped her into bed and snuggled her into their down comforter, she'd been sound asleep. He went alone.

Later, when he got the call to come home the apartment building had burned to the ground. The fire chief told Kelly that the explosion had killed Lynda instantly. She'd never awakened and felt no pain. It was small consolation.

In the aftermath of the tragedy, Kelly quit his job and went out to Indian Creek, where he worked security for the flea market in exchange for a small salary and free rent on a cabin. For the next five years he divided his time between the flea market, Bubba's bait and tackle shop and Cam Belscher's Hideaway Bar. Through the years he slowly began to rebuild his life. He established a small network of friends and eventually came to grips with the devastating loss of his wife.

Two years ago, he decided to make a start on his own social life. He joined a dance club at the Stagecoach in Fort Worth and there he'd met Gillian, a tall blonde with a deep suntan and clear blue eyes. She'd moved over and offered him a spot at the table where she and several of her friends were celebrating someone's birthday. After that Gillian became his favorite dance partner. Eventually he invited her out to the Hideaway, and following one of Cam's famous barbecues, he'd broached the subject of her spending the night. She'd accepted and their relationship had moved to the next level.

For some reason the trip to the Hideaway tonight had stirred up a flood of memories. Maybe it was the peaceful sensation that came over him as he sate at the bar, waiting for Darlene to finish up with the Coors man who'd arrived to stock the coolers. Over in the corner a couple of old timers argued over the points in a never-ending cribbage game, and Johnny Cash walked the line on the jukebox. There was a sameness, but there was a difference.

The murder at Gillian's stables had brought back a lot of those feelings he'd buried following Lynda's death. He hated to admit it, but he was afraid. For the first time in years, he found himself reluctant to stay out at Indian Creek. Gillian needed him—right now for sure—and maybe for longer.

Shaking his head to clear his thoughts, Kelly focused on the interior of the Hideaway. This place was Cam's pride and joy. Stepping inside was like taking a trip down memory lane. The décor—a tribute to the owner's passion for country music and country living—was a potpourri of tools and implements from the turn of the century. In a glass case behind the bar Cam proudly displayed his collection of antique beer wagons—his piece-de-resistance a cherished replica of the Budweiser Clydesdales rigged out in full harness.

Even the ceiling bore witness to Cam's passion. Glossy black and white photos of Hank Williams, Patsy Cline, Faron Young and a whole slew of long-dead country favorites smiled down on the patrons.

* * *

Darlene had just finished with the Coors man and headed down the bar towards Kelly when Jake burst through the front door.

"Hey boy. How's it going?" Kelly crouched into

dog hug position and gave himself over to the pleasure of a full-out canine welcome. "Looks like Darlene's been feeding you plenty." He ran his hands along the dog's fleshy ribs and finished off the greeting with a man to dog head rub.

Darlene had several questions about Bubba's fishing camp, the wedding, and all the other details of his recent holiday. Finally she touched on the subject of the death at Gillian's stables. He was saying goodbye and promising to her updated when his cell phone rang. He flipped it open and Gillian's number flashed across the display.

"Hi Gilly. What's up?"

"Oh my God, Kelly. I'm at the hospital."

"What happened? Are you okay?"

"Yes. It's not me. It's Angelina. When I got to her place the lights were on and the television blaring. But I knocked and knocked on the door and no one answered. I figured maybe she was avoiding me so I called her cell phone.

When she still didn't answer I got worried. That's when I remembered that Sara, Angelina's next door neighbor, had a key. I ran and got Sara and we banged on the door some more. Finally Sara used her key and we found Angelina lying on the floor of her bedroom. She'd been hit over the head, just like Larry. I called 911 and the paramedics showed up in minutes. She's still alive, but barely. I've got to hang up now. The doctor is here."

Kelly had headed for his vehicle while still talking. "I'm on my way." He started the engine and backed onto the road. "I'll call Gus and let him know what's happened."

"Hurry." Gillian sobbed into the receiver.

"I will. Just hang in there." Kelly tossed the phone on the seat and pushed the gas pedal to the floor.

Chapter Three

It took twenty minutes to get to Harris Methodist from Indian Creek with Kelly pushing it all the way. Inside the ER he scanned the room for blondes until his eyes focused on a slim figure huddled into an oversized plastic chair.

"You okay?" He bent over Gillian's chair and lifted her chin to look into her eyes.

"I'm so glad you're here." She lifted her eyes and a teardrop trickled down her cheek."

"Has anyone told you her condition?"

"Yes." Gillian's voice came out as a small squeak. "She's in a coma. The doctor wouldn't give me any details because I'm not family. Angelina's mom and sister just got here. They're meeting with the doctors now." Gillian's voice broke and her shoulders trembled under Kelly's arm.

"You need some coffee." Kelly crouched in front of her chair. "Why don't we take a walk down to the cafeteria. Can you handle a bowl of soup?"

"I couldn't eat, but coffee would be good."

They walked together down the steps and into the gleaming chrome and white cafeteria. Getting some coffee, they took their cups to a quiet corner table. A lush topiary garden screened their table and secluded them from other diners. Kelly waited while Gillian sipped her drink and settled before asking about the events of the morning.

After a short time she set her cup down.

"Angelina lives in one of those cottage apartments on the outskirts of Haltom City. I went straight to her place from the stable."

"Any idea how long it was from the time you left the stable until you called the paramedics?"

"It couldn't have been more than an hour. I drove straight there. Traffic was light. When Angelina didn't answer my knocking, I ran over to Sara's. It didn't take five minutes from the time Sara answered her door until we opened Angelina's."

"Was there any sign something was wrong when you opened the door?"

"No. It was quiet. We walked through the living room back to the bedroom. The door was closed so we knocked a few times. When Angelina didn't answer I opened the door. She was sprawled out on the bed. I thought she was dead at first, but I yelled at Sara to call the paramedics, and then I took her pulse. It was faint, but it was there. Sara went to the door to wait for the medics and I stayed with Angelina."

"Did it look like Angelina had put up a fight?"

"Not at all. Whoever did this must have caught her sleeping. The room hadn't been disturbed and there were no signs of a struggle."

"What about Sara, did you ask if she'd heard anything out of the ordinary before you arrived?"

"Yes. The walls aren't that thick in the complex and Sara is positive she'd have heard if there'd been a struggle. She and Angelina both live alone, so they've a pact to look out for each other. If Sara had heard anything that sounded like an attack on Angelina she'd have investigated. "

Thirty minutes dragged like thirty hours as they waited for news. When Kelly's phone buzzed he stepped outside to answer. It was Gus.

"Any news?"

"No. She's still in a coma. The doctor's with the mother and sister now. There's something I need to say though. I'm afraid I might have screwed up."

"How's that?"

"I overheard Angelina and one of the boys in the barn earlier this evening. They were talking about someone named Sam who apparently knows something about Larry's death."

"God damn it Kelly. You know better than to sit on something like that."

"I know it Gus. I've been kicking my own ass ever since Gillian's call. It's a bit different though, not being official. I wanted to show Gilly some respect, let her talk to the girl. Besides I figured she'd get more out of Angelina than I would. That's why Gillian went over there tonight. To find out what she knew."

"Well it's too late to cry now. What about this Sam? Does Gillian know him?"

"No. She knows who he is, but she doesn't know anything about him."

"How about the boy Angelina was talking to?"

"I don't know. It could be any one of the five that work there. The voices were whispered and he didn't ring any bells. You're going to want to talk to all of them. I know them all, casually, and I tried to pin down the voice but nothing stuck."

"Okay. We'll save that for later. I'm on my way over there now. I'll put a man on the girl's door. Nobody in or out except family and Gillian."

"Thanks. It'll help if you let the doctor know that I'm assisting. Right now he's not speaking to anyone except family."

"I'll talk to him. See you in ten."

Back inside Kelly found Gillian with an older woman who had to be Angelina's mother, and the sister, a girl of about fourteen.

"Kelly, this is Mrs. Morales and Juanita," Gillian performed introductions.

"I'm so sorry about Angelina." Kelly covered the older woman's hand with his own. "Did the doctor have any idea how long she might be unconscious?"

"He doesn't know." She sobbed. "He says there might be brain damage. They can't tell yet. Why would anyone hurt my Angelina? She's a good girl. She's never in trouble. All she does is work and study. Ms. Gillian will tell you. Angelina is never in trouble."

"Please, Mrs. Morales, we know she hasn't done anything wrong. What we're afraid of is that Angelina saw or heard something, something to do with the young boy who was murdered last night."

"But she didn't know anything about that. I called her this morning. She said she didn't know anything. She promised me she didn't know why the boy was killed. My Angelina is a good girl."

"You must be Juanita." Kelly turned to the young girl who stood behind her mother.

Brown eyes widened and she ducked her head

shyly.

"Did you ever hear your sister mention the name Sam?"

"I don't think so."

"Have you ever seen your sister with any of the boys from the stable?"

The girl darted a look at her mother and then looked at Gillian.

"It's okay Juanita." Gillian reached out and took the girl's hand. "We only want to find out who might have hurt Angelina. Anything you tell us that will help catch whoever did this will be helping to protect your sister."

"She sometimes went walking with the boy who was killed."

"No!" Mrs. Morales wailed.

Juanita cowered at the shout from her mother, but she stiffened her shoulders and nodded her head yes.

"She did Mama. She knew you didn't like him, so she met him in secret. She made me promise not to tell you when slipped out to meet him. Angelina said they were just friends, but I followed her one night and I saw her kiss him."

"Thank you Juanita." Gillian jumped in before the woman could scold her daughter. "You've been very helpful to your sister and we really appreciate your honesty. I know your mom understands that you were only protecting Angelina."

Gillian placed her arm around the older woman's shoulder. After a moment of composure Mrs. Morales reached out and embraced her daughter.

The sound of heavy footsteps outside the small

visitor's room announced the arrival of Gus and two uniformed officers. Kelly left the women and joined Gus in the hallway. "Any news?" Gus asked.

"Angelina is in a deep coma and according to the doctor they have no idea when or if she will regain consciousness."

"That bad. I'll go have a talk with the doctor. This is Deputy Raymond," Gus indicated the tallest of the officers standing to his right, "and Deputy Williams," he motioned towards the shorter of the two. "They'll be on the door in alternating four hour shifts."

"Glad to meet you Deputy Raymond, Deputy Williams," Kelly shook hands with the men and fell into step with Gus who led the men to the nurse's station. He introduced them to the charge nurse and inquired about the doctor's whereabouts.

"It's Dr. Winchester," the nurse told Gus. "He's probably doing his charts. It's four doors down on the left. You can catch him there."

They found Dr. Winchester bent over a pile of charts. Gus made introductions and explained that the two officers would remain on duty outside Angelina's door for the foreseeable future.

The doctor confirmed the girl's diagnosis and promised to contact Gus if there was any change. Gus also cleared Kelly and Gillian for access to Angelina's room.

"I'm going to tackle those kids first thing in the morning," Gus said, as he and Kelly headed for the elevators.

"Great. I need to take Gillian home now.

Hopefully she'll get a few hours sleep. I'll stay out there tonight, and if it's okay I'll join you in the morning."

"Good. You know most of those kids. That should help establish a rapport, and hopefully you'll spot anything hinky."

Kelly and Gus parted at the elevator and Kelly returned to the visitor's lounge.

"Gus and I have spoken with the doctor," he told Gillian. "Things are just as Mrs. Morales described them. I think, and the doctor agrees, that everyone should go home now and get some sleep."

"But shouldn't I stay with Angelina?" Mrs. Morales was obviously looking to Kelly for guidance.

"The nurses will take good care of Angelina. It's you and Juanita we need to worry about now. The doctor explained that this is going to be a long haul. It won't help Angelina if you get yourself sick."

"Kelly's right." Gillian said to the older woman. "Did you drive or do you need us to drop you off?"

"We came in a taxi. I'm going to call my husband to come and get us after he gets off work. He'll want to sit with Angelina for awhile, and then, as you say, we'll all go home and get some rest."

"Excellent." Kelly patted the older woman's arm and then turned to Gillian. "Are you ready to go home now? I think we could all use some rest."

"Yes. I'm ready. Mrs. Morales, you'll call me if you need anything won't you?"

"Of course. Thank you so much."

Kelly and Gillian headed for the Jeep in the parking lot. They hadn't gone a mile before Gillian dropped off to sleep with her head resting on Kelly's shoulder.

At the ranch, Kelly opened the door on Gillian's side of the Jeep and picked her up in his arms.

"You don't have to carry me. I can walk." She mumbled an objection.

"Shhh! Humor me, okay? You've had enough for one day. Close your eyes and I'll have you undressed and tucked in before you have a chance to blink."

* * *

The next morning Gus arrived while Kelly was on the porch having coffee.

"I've got your cup right here." Kelly said, as Gus mounted the steps. "Gillian's out at the stables. I said I'd let her know when you arrived. She'll send the stable hands in, one at a time, whenever you're ready. You can fix a couple of biscuits while I tell her you're here."

"I can handle that." Gus pulled up a chair, poured a cup from the steaming carafe and reached into the basket for a couple of Gillian's buttermilk biscuits.

At the barn, Kelly found Gillian and two of the workers forking hay from the loft down into the mangers.

"Gus is here and ready whenever you are," he called up.

Gillian poked her head over the railing. "Can you give us another ten? We've just about filled the mangers. Mike and I will start grooming and Kevin can go talk to Gus."

"Sounds good."

Back at the house Gus had polished off the basket of biscuits and settled into his chair with a fresh cup of coffee.

"They're just finishing with the hay. Gilly will send Kevin along first. He should be here in ten minutes or so. Did you get enough coffee?"

"Plenty. I made short work of those biscuits. If I don't see the chef, be sure and give her my compliments."

Kelly laughed. "Gillian will like that."

Kelly settled down beside Gus in the other oversize deck chair. They sipped coffee in the peaceful dawn.

"How's Jake been keeping?" Gus asked.

"I don't think that old shepherd is ever going to slow down. He's frisky as a pup. I stopped by the Hideaway last night and he about knocked me off the porch."

"He was probably letting you know he'd had enough of being a house guest."

"Don't I know it. It's been nice of Darlene to keep him, but with all her cats I've a feeling my name is probably Mud in dog lingo."

"Oh God yeah. She must have half a dozen of those fur balls hanging around."

"I'm planning to stay with Gillian for the time being. I'll run out to the Creek and pick Jake up later tonight."

"I like the idea of you staying here until we figure out what this killer's all about. It might, as I know you realize, be about drugs, but it doesn't smell right."

"I agree. I've been out of the racket for quite

awhile now, but I think I'd recognize the signs, something you never forget. This one doesn't fit. I thought I'd call a couple of the guys I knew back in the day and run the names of these kids by them. If there's anything to do with drugs going on, one of those names is bound to pop. That is if you don't have any objection?"

"Not at all. I was working up to asking if you were comfortable getting in touch with some of your old contacts."

At that point a tall skinny kid with sandy hair and a mouthful of braces opened the gate and approached the two men on the porch.

"Gillian said you wanted to see me." The young lad climbed the steps and stopped in front of Gus. "I'm Kevin Holmes."

"How are you Kevin?" Gus shook hands and motioned towards Kelly. "I guess you know Kelly McWinter."

"Yes sir." He nodded at Kelly and turned his head back to Gus.

"Make yourself comfortable." Gus motioned to one of the chairs and waited while Kevin perched himself tentatively on the edge of the seat.

"Of course you realize we're inquiring into the death of one of your co-workers. I think the best way to approach this is for you to tell us as much as you can about Larry and anything in his life that might have precipitated the kind of violence that led to his death."

"We weren't really buds. I just kind of knew him from work. He was okay, but kind of, I don't know, flaky I guess you'd call it."

"What do you mean by flaky?"

"Well, for instance, he didn't like to work too much, so if we took in a new horse or something came up that meant we'd have a busy day, he'd probably get sick and not come in that day. Stuff like that."

"Okay. How about his relationship with the others? Did he get along? With Larry being a slacker is it possible he made someone angry enough to start a fight?"

"Nah, nothing like that. He wasn't a regular, you know, just a casual. We all liked Robin better, but she's a girl." Kevin grinned a bit and then ducked his head back down.

"So as far as you know there wasn't anything to do with the job that might have led to violence?"

"No sir. Nothing. I don't guess any of us considered Larry a pal, but nobody hated him either."

"What about Larry's friends. Did you know any of them?"

"No. Sorry, like I said, we weren't buds."

"All right. Thank you Kevin. Anything else you can think of that might be worth checking. It doesn't have to relate just to Larry. What I'm looking for is anything that might have seemed unusual, out of the ordinary."

"Well. You mean like Angelina telling Sam he wasn't allowed to come around the stables when Gillian wasn't home?"

"That's exactly what I mean. Who is this Sam? And when did Angelina run him off?"

"I think he's a friend of Clinton, Larry's brother.

I don't usually work on Saturday but Robin had a test to study for so she asked me if I'd take her shift."

"And that's when you met Sam?"

"That's right. Larry and I were mucking out the barn. It was about eleven-thirty when he showed up. Larry said they were supposed to have lunch and did I mind if he knocked off early. I told him he needed to help me finish the mucking out first. Like I said before, he always tried to get out of the crappy jobs."

"Was it because Larry wasn't getting his work done that Angelina told Sam he'd have to leave?"

"Nope. Sam went over and sat at the break table while Larry and I finished the mucking out. Angelina was in the office, but she came out to the barn for something and that's when she got into it with Sam. I didn't really hear what they said, just the last part, when Angelina told him to get out. She yelled at him, and that was unusual. Angelina never raises her voice to anyone."

"What about Larry. Do you think he knew what Angelina was upset about?"

"Maybe you should ask Angelina about that." Kevin's face flushed and he dropped his eyes to stare at his hands.

Gus left it alone. "We'll be talking to Angelina this evening. Anything else?"

"No sir. Nothing."

"Would you mind sending Mike along when you get back to the barn." Gus stood up to indicate the interview was over and Kevin hurried down the steps and out the gate to the stable yard.

"Well that was interesting." Kelly stretched his

long legs and shifted around in the chair. "Gives a bit more credence to our drug theory."

* * *

Mike turned out to be the antithesis of Kevin. Short and pudgy, with curly brown hair and an easy grin, the young man said hi to Kelly, introduced himself to Gus and settled comfortably into the chair vacated by Kevin.

"I told the others Larry didn't off himself." Mike's nose twitched like a weasel scenting food. "I guess you being here means its murder, right?"

Gus scowled. "We're doing a preliminary investigation. Suppose you tell us everything you know about what happened on Saturday."

"Well. I wasn't here, of course. But there's been talk. Larry was kind of a rotter. I suppose you've found that out." Mike kept his eyes fixed on Gus while he talked. "I'm a criminology student, you know. This the first opportunity I've had to get in on the ground floor, so to speak, in an investigation. I've been asking questions right and left."

"That so." Gus squinted a bit, and Kelly knew he was taking Mike's measure, deciding how much room he wanted to give the kid.

"Find out anything useful?" he asked.

Mike's eyes lit up. Apparently Gus had decided he might be helpful and you'd have thought the boy had struck gold.

"Toby probably won't like it that I've told you this, but its murder, right?"

Mike paused, hoping for confirmation, but Gus waved for him to continue and the boy went on with his story.

"It was Sunday morning. Toby came in to work and found Larry sleeping one off in the manger."

"Was Larry supposed to be there on Sunday?"

"No. Toby and Robin work Sundays. Larry knows he's not supposed to hang around the stables when he isn't working, but Miss Gillian was out of town and Larry liked pushing his luck."

"Okay. So Larry was sleeping it off in the stables. I assume he and Toby had a conversation that might be relevant to Larry's death."

"That's right." Mike flashed a huge grin and nodded his head up and down.

"According to Toby, Larry had been out partying Friday night, and since he was scheduled to work Saturday morning, he decided to crash in the barn. Like I said, he knew Ms. Gillian was out of town.

"Then what?"

"Early Saturday morning Larry heard loud voices coming from down below in the barn. As soon as he realized that a couple of people were having an argument, Larry crawled over to the edge of the manger to see who was talking."

"And did he find out?"

"Yep. It was Sam, a friend of Larry's brother Clinton. Of course that piqued Larry's interest, because Sam is a drug dealer, just small time, but Larry figured if he eavesdropped maybe he'd find out enough to get himself a stash."

"And the second person?"

"Dr. Morgan, the Veterinarian who looks after Miss Gillian's horses. Larry couldn't hear it all, but it sounded like Sam was threatening the doctor."

"Did he say what kind of threat?"

"He wasn't sure. He heard something about Percocet – that's what Larry got Larry's attention – and then their voices got low, and then Sam said, "you either come through or I'll be spreading it around."

"Did either of them realize that Larry was in the hayloft?"

"The doctor didn't. He told Sam he'd see him later and left. Larry figured he was clear, but once the doctor left Sam yelled at Larry to get his ass down from the hayloft."

"Do you think Sam was mad enough to do Larry an injury?"

"No. Sam's a punk, but he's not a killer. Besides, Larry said Sam claimed he'd misunderstood the conversation."

"How's that?"

"According to Sam he and the doctor were arguing about the medication the doctor had given Sam's friend for his horse. Apparently the doctor had given his friend Percocet, but the horse died. Sam's friend wanted a refund but the doctor said he had to pay for the medicine even if it didn't work."

"What did Larry think about that?"

"He still thought something was fishy, but he pretended to accept Sam's explanation. Then, according to Toby, Larry went to the office to see Angelina. He's got a bad crush on her, and I guess he figured if he couldn't get anything out of Sam he'd use the information to get on the good side of Angelina.

"What did Angelina have to say?"

"She told Larry that seeing as how Gillian's boyfriend was a detective." Mike grinned over at Kelly. "They should wait until Gillian returned and tell her everything so she could decide what needed to be done."

"And that was the last time Toby talked to Larry?"

"No. Not quite. Larry told Toby that after he'd talked to Angelina, he went back to the barn and went to work. It was towards the end of the day when the doctor showed up at the barn to tend to one of the horses."

Both Gus and Kelly perked up at the mention of the doctor's return.

Mike shifted in his chair and smiled, apparently pleased to have recaptured their attention.

"Toby told me that Larry was still bugged about Sam's story so he decided to quiz the doctor."

"Not the brightest kid on the planet," Kelly muttered.

"Nope. Anyway, the doctor backed up Sam's story, and when Larry told him that he'd told his girlfriend Angelina about the conversation, he accused Larry of being a trouble making little rat. Said he'd discuss it with Gillian himself, and for Larry to get the hell out of his sight. "

Mike looked from Gus to Kelly and beamed at both of them. "I guess you'll want to be talking to the doctor now?"

Gus stood up. "You've been very helpful. As a

criminology student I'm sure you'll appreciate the importance of keeping the information you've given us confidential."

"Oh sure." Mike jumped up from his chair and nodded his head vigorously. "I won't say a word. You can count on my discretion."

"Thank you. We'll be in touch." Gus said, and Mike reluctantly headed back to the barn.

"He sure would have like to tag along when you went to question the doctor." Kelly laughed when Gus gave him a scowl.

"Just what I need. Wet nursing. I've got to admit the kid gave us some interesting information."

"I imagine the doctor's at the top of your agenda. Would you like me to check with Toby and see what he has to say about Mike's story?"

"That'd be good. Why don't you follow up that end while I go have a few words with the good doctor."

Chapter Four

Gillian flopped into the chair beside Kelly and pressed her fingers to her eyelids.

"Headache?"

"It just started. I've taken some Advil, hopefully it'll work."

Kelly rose from his chair and circled behind hers. "Let me give it a try." He placed his hands on her shoulders and gently worked his thumbs into the chords along her neck.

"That's heavenly." She let her head fall back and breathed deep.

""Let's see if we can work out some of those kinks." Kelly kneaded her neck and shoulders, rubbing gently and then adding more pressure, until gradually the tension seeped out and she slumped back in her chair.

"Thank you," she whispered capturing his mouth in hers when he bent over and found her lips.

"I know an even better headache remedy," Kelly said, raising his eyebrows and giving her his best imitation of Simon Legree.

"I bet you do, and when I get done work tonight I'm going to expect a personal demonstration."

"You're on." Kelly settled back into his chair. "Now, tell me about Toby. Would you consider him a reliable witness?"

Gillian frowned. "Surely he isn't mixed up in this

mess. He's one of my regulars you know."

"I don't think he's necessary mixed up in anything, but it looks like he has information that he hasn't been forthcoming about."

"What kind of information?"

"According to Mike, Larry overheard Sam trying to blackmail your vet into supplying him with Percocet."

"Dr. Morgan? That's ridiculous. Why in heaven's name would Dr. Morgan get involved with Sam Taylor? He's a respectable veterinarian and Sam Taylor's a punk."

"That's what Gus is trying to find out. He left a few minutes ago for the doctor's clinic. In the meantime he asked me to verify Toby's story. I thought you might have his home address in your files."

"Yes, of course. I just don't understand any of this. Toby is a very responsible boy. I can't imagine him having anything to do with drugs or murder."

"He might not. All we know at this point is that he supposedly overheard something. Don't forget this was relayed to us second hand by Mike."

"I know. Mike's another one of my regular hands. I can't believe he didn't come to me if he had information about something wrong at the stables."

"Hang on, now. Remember you've been on vacation. Probably the kids were trying to protect you. Besides, apparently Toby told Angelina, and she was going to talk to you about it herself."

"I feel so guilty. If I hadn't been gone, Angelina wouldn't be in the hospital and maybe none of this would have happened."

Kelly stood and reached down to pull Gillian out

of her chair. He wrapped her into his arms. "You can't think that way. First, we don't know if the story Toby and Mike are telling has anything to do with Larry's murder. Secondly, what happened to Angelina would likely have happened rather you were here or not. You know how kids are. They protect one another. Even the best of them. It sounds to me like Angelina was trying to give Sam an opportunity to do the right thing. Angelina would have been in danger whether you'd been here or not. It was protecting her friends that put her in harm's way, not you being on vacation."

Gillian leaned her head on Kelly's shoulder and sighed. "I suppose you're right. I just feel so impotent. All this stuff happening right under my nose and I never suspected a thing."

"Come on. Let's not jump to conclusions. The first thing we need to do is have a talk with Toby. Why don't you go get his address and we'll drive out there together. Does that suit?"

"Yes. Please. I want to know exactly what Toby overheard and I want you there with me so there won't be any misunderstanding."

"Good. You get his address and I'll pull the Jeep around front."

* * *

"He lives over near the Stockyards, on Bonnie Bray Avenue. It's just off East Belknap." Gillian handed Kelly a neatly printed address card.

He noted the address, and recognized the

location. "That's about fifteen minutes away. We'll get there at dinner time and with luck catch him home. Once we get confirmation on the story Kevin told Gus, we'll have a better idea what kind of mess we're dealing with."

"Good. I'm scared Kelly. We need to find out what's going on before anyone else gets hurt, or worse."

"Don't worry. Gus is the best, and I know a few things about criminal investigations myself. We'll get to the bottom of this."

"I don't know what I'd do without you."

"You're not going to have to worry about that either. I'm here for the duration. This is the 3000 block, keep an eye out for Bonnie Brae, it's on your side."

Kelly cruised as slow as traffic allowed until Gillian called out.

"That's it." She pointed towards a street sign and Kelly braked for a quick right turn.

Half way up the block he pulled up in front of a white house with blue shutters and a small but attractive front yard, and turned off the Jeep. "Do you want me to wait here while you see if he's home?"

"Yes, thanks. It might spook him if we both show up on his doorstep. I'll tell him we have some questions that he needs to answer and bring him out."

"Good idea. That way we can talk to him alone."

Kelly watched Gillian as she crossed the yard and climbed the steps to the front porch. She pressed the doorbell and waited. After a few minutes she pressed again. Finally the door opened and a gray haired woman in a summery print dress peeked around the door, asked a question and then swung the door open inviting Gillian inside.

Several minutes passed and Kelly was getting ready to go check on things, when the door opened once again and Gillian started down the path, alone.

Must be out somewhere. Kelly muttered. "No luck?" he queried, when Gillian opened the door and climbed back in the Jeep.

"Worse than that. He's disappeared."

"What?"

"His mom hasn't seen him since Sunday night and she's fit to be tied."

"Did he say anything about going anywhere?"

"No. He got up Sunday morning and went to work, like usual. That's the last she saw of him."

"So he never came home from work."

"That's the problem. She worked in her garden until dinner time. Toby usually got off work about four o'clock and she figured he'd gone to his room for a nap."

"Was that usual?"

"She says yes. His room's upstairs and when she came in from the garden she fixed dinner and then called him down. When he didn't answer, she went upstairs and that's when she discovered he was gone."

"Did she notice anything missing?"

"Not then, but when he still hadn't come home the next morning, she checked his closet and his duffle bag was missing."

"Was he in the habit of taking off without letting her know?"

"She says not. She's a widow, and he knows she worries so he always tells her if he's going to be gone overnight. I don't like it Kelly."

"I know. I don't like it myself, but let's not jump to conclusions. He's a teenager, stuff happens when you're that age. Did you ask if he has a girlfriend?"

"Yes I did. His mom said there was a girl at school he dated once in awhile, but he didn't have a steady girlfriend."

"Well that's a start. Did you get the address?"

"Of course."

"Atta girl. I'll give Gus a call and we'll head on over there. I don't suppose Toby's mom has called the police?"

"Actually she did, but they told her he hadn't been gone forty-eight hours, and she should relax, he was probably out partying with his friends and he'd be back as soon as he sobered up."

"I bet she loved that."

"She's not too happy with our civil servants right now."

"Of course you realize they're very likely right and that's exactly what has happened."

"I hope so Kelly, but I'm worried. Do you mind if we stop by the hospital next? I talked to Mrs. Morales this morning and she told me the doctor said there was no change in Angelina's condition. I know there's nothing I can do, but I'd like to see her for myself."

"We'll head over there now. I can call Gus while you're talking to Mrs. Morales. Maybe he's found out something that'll give us a lead on Toby's whereabouts."

* * *

At the hospital Kelly pulled up to the main entrance. "Take your time," he told Gillian. "I'm going to pull up in the shade of that old pecan tree and give Gus a call. You spend as long as you like with Mrs. Morales."

"Thanks." Gillian scooted over and kissed him on the cheek. "You're a prince."

"Hey, surely a prince is entitled to more than a peck."

"We'll talk about it later."

Kelly swung around to the back of the lot and pulled up beneath the big old tree.

Pretty good harvest. Kelly pushed open the door of the jeep and moved aside a branch loaded with nuts so he could stretch his legs. Once he'd gotten comfortable he took his cell out of its holder on the visor and touched Gus' number.

"Yo. It's me," he said, when Gus' growl came through the speaker. "Any luck with the vet?"

"Nothing. I tried telling him we had information that he'd been supplying drugs to the kids at the stable, but the old bastard was either innocent or smart. He claimed some idiot named Sam came to the stable and asked for Oxycontin to treat the sick horse of a friend."

"Do you think he was giving it to you straight?"

"Sounded plausible. He's a hell of a lot more credible than any of those kids. I gave him Mike's version of the story and he said it was a crock. Claims he ran them both out of the stable and told them he planned to tell Gillian what they were up to first chance he got."

Sounds like the Doc's story is a lot more

plausible than Mike's. Kelly mused after he'd hung up from his conversation with Gus.

Time to put in some leg work.

He got out of the truck and headed into the hospital, where he located Gillian sitting with Mrs. Morales.

"Did Gus know anything?" She asked meeting Kelly at the door to the waiting room.

Kelly shook his head. "Far as I can tell it's another dead end. He completely disputed Mike's version of Toby's story. The Doc claims he ran Sam out of the stables when he tried to con him out of some Oxycontin. He told Gus he planned on reporting Sam to you first chance he got, but he's been tied up with a sick horse."

"That makes a lot more sense to me than Mike's story." Gillian nodded her head. "What do you and Gus think?"

"Same as you. It doesn't figure that a smart doctor is going to get involved with a bunch of scatterbrained kids. Unless, of course, there's something more behind all of this." Kelly frowned. "I'm keeping an open mind, of course, but I think it's time to call in a few favors. I still have a couple of contacts from my undercover days. I'll have to take you home though. Where I'm going is definitely no place for a lady."

Gillian laughed. "I guess that means you don't think I could pass myself off as a biker chick."

"I don't recall mentioning bikers."

Gillian rolled her eyes and tossed her head. "Okay. Be mysterious. I'll go say goodbye to Mrs. Morales. You can drop me off at the stables and I'll get some work done while you go pursue your nefarious activities."

Women. Kelly muttered jovially as Gillian headed off to say her goodbyes.

* * *

After smoothing Gillian's ruffled feathers as best he could and dropping her at the stables, Kelly headed for Texas B's on Belknap. In keeping with the early hour, the parking lot held a couple of bikes a battered pickup and an old Chrysler that Kelly recognized as belonging to longtime bar manager, Fred Todd.

That's a lucky break. Kelly's spirits rose when he spotted the Chrysler. Back in his undercover days he had come to Fred's rescue on a Monday night when three rowdy Bandits rolled into town and started giving the barman a hard time.

It had been early on a stormy night. The members of the Texas Brothers, a local motorcycle club that called the bar home base, had been holding it's annual membership meeting. Kelly, in his undercover persona of Jake, had been chatting with the bartender in the mostly empty bar, and except for the two of them and a local wino, the place had been deserted.

"That was a short meeting," Fred had commented when motorcycle engines roared up to the front entrance.

Moments later a group of three bikers decked out in Bandit colors shoved open the door and swaggered up to the bar.

"Got any beer in this deadhead joint?" A loud mouth with a bandana wrapped around his greasy blond hair slammed his fist down on the bar and aimed a "dare you" glare in Kelly's direction.

His two buddies, a burly black man and a tall skinny Latino slid onto stools on either side of their buddy.

"What'll you have?" Fred asked walking down the bar and wiping the counter in front of the three men.

"Three Buds. And since we're new in town and checking this place out, you can give them to us on the house."

"Sorry." Fred shook his head. "We don't give out no freebies."

"This is one of those times you might want to make an exception." The loud mouth stood up and leaned over the bar towards Fred.

Fred swiveled his head in Kelly's direction. "No exceptions," he muttered, backing away from the group.

"You boys new in town?" Kelly stood up from his seat at the end of the bar and strolled towards the group. As he walked he let his jacket fall back far enough for a discerning eye to catch the bulge made by the revolver tucked in the waistband of his jeans.

"Guess your hearing's pretty good." Loud mouth swiveled to Kelly but made no move to step forward.

"Sure is." Kelly kept moving forward. "Far as I can tell, you boys are flying Bandit colors. Seemed a bit strange being this is the Brotherhood's stomping grounds." Kelly pointed towards a group photo that Fred had displayed behind the cash register.

Loud mouth's black companion leaned forward

and squinted at the large group of Brotherhood members all proudly flying their colors.

"Don't seem like anyone's marking territory tonight." The black fellow muttered.

"Not at the moment." Kelly grinned. "Like Fred said, the Brothers don't hold with giving out no free samples. The boys are holding a meeting right now. They'll be done with business in about half an hour. They'll all be piling in here shortly, and depending on how the meeting went – you boys know how those things are – they'll either be feeling really sociable, or not. Sound about right to you Fred?"

"That's right. You boys want me to set you up, you can pay for your beer now and once the Brothers get here I can let them know you'd like a welcome to Fort Worth and maybe they'll reimburse your money."

The expression on all three faces made it clear they knew damn good and well what kind of welcome they could expect.

Loud mouth slid off his stool. "We'll be back later once you've got some business in this joint." He yanked his thumb towards the door, and the other two followed him outside.

"Damn, I'd never have thought of that if you hadn't spoken up, I sure appreciate your help." The bartender had been all over Kelly with gratitude. "You ever find yourself in need of a favor, don't hesitate to ask." Kelly, as Jake, had never taken Fred up on his offer, but this seemed like a good time to test the bartender's memory.

* * *

"Jake, where the hell have you been? What's it been three or four years?" Fred reached across the bar and pumped Kelly's hand like a long lost friend.

"How's it going Fred," Kelly returned the handshake. "I moved out to the country a few years ago. Don't get back into town very often nowadays."

"Ah, sounds like you got yourself shacked up out in the sticks. Must be something special the way you're keeping to yourself."

Kelly grinned. "Yeah. Guess I'm getting old. How's business?"

"Not too bad. Course times have changed. A lot of the old timers have moved on or changed directions. Not many flying colors anymore. Still, we do okay."

"Good to hear. I was hoping to see a few familiar faces."

"Well, let's see, Stan's still around, and Mike and Ron. Like I said a lot of them have moved on or moved away."

Kelly nodded. "Yep, times change. I was kind of looking for some information for a friend of mine. Maybe you can help."

"Anything I know is yours, Jake. Like I told you before, I owe you, and I don't forget my debts."

"Thanks Fred, but this ain't a big deal. Just a favor for a friend. Apparently his kid's gotten into a bit of a mess, and my friend's worried the kid may have gotten involved with the wrong kind of folks. He asked me if I still had any connections out on the street." Kelly grinned. "I'm afraid I'm about as out of touch as it's possible to be, but I figured the Brothers would be sure to know if anything was shaking on their home ground."

"What's the deal?"

"Best I can tell it's got to do with new drug territory opening up and maybe a new outfit moving in."

"Here in town?"

"Apparently this involves dealing in schools and junior colleges—high end prescription drugs and that kind of shit."

Fred shook his head. "You remember the Brothers steered clear of that kind of action. They weren't above growing a few plants, but what you're talking about sounds more like them Bandit sons-of-bitches."

"That's what I thought too. I wonder if maybe Phil or Ron might know anything. Wasn't Ron involved in a wrestling club that had a few Bandit members?"

"Wouldn't hurt to ask. I don't know if he's wrestling anymore, packed on too many pounds, but he still hangs around there and I think he does a bit of coaching."

"It's a possibility at least. Here's my cell number." Kelly scribbled his number on a piece of paper and handed it over. "I'd sure appreciate it if you'd pick the big man's brain next time he's in here and give me a call with whatever you manage to find out."

"So you want to know if he's heard anything about a high end drug lord moving into town, and anything he might have heard about the operation."

"Yep. And, while you're at it, ask him if these people, whoever they are, have anything to do with horses or horse racing?"

"Say, didn't I hear about a murder out at one of those Lake Country riding stables the other day?"

Kelly nodded his head. "The lady who owns the place is by way of being a friend of a friend of mine. She's worried about what some of the young people working out there might have gotten themselves involved in, so I've promised my friend that I'd see what I could find out."

"Okay. Like as not Ron will be in later tonight. I'll see what I can find out and give you a call in the morning."

"Thanks Fred. Nice seeing you again."

"Yeah. Same here."

Fred went to look after a customer who had entered the bar and Kelly headed back to his truck.

Might as well check in with Gus. He pulled out of the parking lot and headed for downtown. He'd gone about four blocks when his cell buzzed, and Kelly punched the hands free.

"Kelly, where you at right now?" Gus' voice came over the speaker.

"Enroute to the station. Figured on comparing notes. Why? Something happen."

"You might say that. Why don't you detour by the White Bull. I'll catch you up while we're grabbing a bite."

"On my way." Kelly clicked off the phone and headed for Jacksboro Highway. Must be something big for Gus not to share the news over the phone. Course he's got a cop's distrust for open airwaves.

* * *

"So what's up?" Kelly slid into the booth across from Gus and took the cup of coffee from Ruby, their regular waitress, who had followed him down the aisle to their favorite booth at the back of the busy diner.

"Thanks. I'll have the usual." Kelly smiled at Ruby before turning his attention back to Gus.

"Toby's dead. A couple of fishermen spotted his body in Eagle Mountain Lake. Looks like someone dumped him into the Trinity Sunday night and the current took him down river to the lake where he got caught up in one of those weed beds."

"Damn."

"Yeah. Did you have any luck with your old contacts?

"Nothing concrete. There's a possibility one or two of the Bandits might know something, but it'll be tricky. I've left messages for a couple of guys from the old days. Hopefully one or both of them will get in touch."

Kelly's biscuits loaded with sausage gravy had arrived while they talked and for several minutes both men concentrated on their plates.

"Guess we'll just have to keep digging." Gus reached for the bill and pulled some cash out of his pocket. "My turn for this. I need to get back to the station. You'll keep in touch, right?"

"You bet. I'm going to run out to Indian Creek and rescue Jake from Darlene's cats. I'll spend some more time with Gillian's stable hands see if I can pick up anything we missed."

"Sounds good." Gus headed for the till leaving Kelly to finish his last swallows of coffee.

Sitting back, his brow creased in thought, Kelly sipped and let his mind run back over everything he'd seen and heard since returning from Oregon. *I'm missing something.* Kelly sifted through his mind, examining unconnected thoughts and snatches of conversation in hopes that some kind of pattern might emerge.

Best leave it for awhile. It'll surface. He tucked a couple of bills under his cup and stood just as his cell buzzed. Kelly flipped open the case and Gillian's number flashed on the display.

"Just leaving," he said. "You want to take a run out to the Hideaway while I pick up Jake?"

"Angelina's awake. She wants to talk to you."

"I'll be there in ten." Kelly stuck the phone in his pocket and headed for the door. Finally, it looked like they were going to get some answers. He'd check in with Gillian first and then give Gus a call.

Chapter Five

At Harris Methodist Kelly parked in the short term lot and called Gillian on her cell.

"I'll meet you in the Atrium," she said. "They aren't allowing visitors, but Angelina's mom got me in for a few minutes and I think I have some answers for you."

"Be right there."

Gillian had obviously stopped for coffee because when Kelly came through the door she handed over one of the Starbucks she was holding.

"Let's grab a seat by the window, and I'll bring you up to date."

On the far side of the Atrium's cheerful oasis of lush greenery and blooming tropical plants, they found a private table for two and sat down with their coffee.

"How's she doing?" Kelly asked.

"She's out of the coma and she remembers the attack. They're still running tests, and they'll probably keep her for a few days, but there doesn't seem to be any permanent damage."

"That's great. So what did she tell you?"

"She didn't recognize her attacker, but she did see him. Unfortunately he had a black hoodie over his head and a scarf covering his face. She said he was male, six feet tall, and his hands were old. But remember, he'd seem like a giant to a frightened girl, and thirty-five would be old to a teenager."

"True, but that does tell us it wasn't one of the kids from the stable."

"Yes. Thank God. It's the first thing I asked her. She's positive it wasn't anyone she knows."

"Okay. So now the big question, did she tell you what she was hiding?"

"Yes. Like you suspected, it was drugs. Sam is apparently an old buddy of Larry's brother Clinton. It seems that Clinton decided to move out to the West Coast a couple months ago, and Sam started hanging around with Larry. He'd show up at school and take Larry and his friends for rides in his car, stuff like that. Of course, what Sam was looking for was a market for his drugs."

"Bastard. So Larry introduced Sam to all his buddies and Sam started supplying. What was he pushing, did Angelina know?"

"Ecstasy and cocaine she thought, maybe Meth."

"Okay, so why would someone kill Larry?"

"Angelina claims she had convinced Larry to come clean with me as soon as we got back from Oregon. She thinks Larry must have told Sam he was going to squeal and Sam's supplier had him murdered."

"Which implies Larry was an innocent bystander who was meaning to do the right thing, and that doesn't exactly jive with what we've been hearing from the other kids."

"I know, but Angelina had a crush on Larry, she wanted to believe him."

"I take it he did not tell her the name of Sam's supplier?"

"She claims he didn't know."

"Did you ask her about Dr. Morgan?"

"Yes. Larry never mentioned him. I asked Angelina what she thought of the doctor and she said he was 'kind of creepy' but he was good with the horses. For what it's worth, that's my take as well."

"Fits with Gus' report too. We'll keep him in mind though."

Kelly slipped his arm around Gillian's shoulders and gave her a hug. "I know this isn't easy and I appreciate you asking Angelina all these questions."

Gillian rested her head on his shoulder, her eyes bright with unshed tears. "Do you want to question her, just in case I missed something?"

"Not now. You've done a fine job. Likely Gus will want to talk to her when she's feeling better, but let's leave her with family for now. Do you need a ride back to the stables?"

"No, I brought my car. I'm going to take Mrs. Morales home. She's been here since last night. I'll drive her so she doesn't have to catch a bus."

They stood and walked together back to the main lobby.

"You going to be okay?" Kelly asked.

"I'll be fine." Gillian raised on her toes and pressed her lips to his. "I hate it that all this was happening around me and I was totally unaware. You can bet it won't happen again. My staff and I are going to be having some serious heart-to-hearts, and if I don't like their answers I'll be doing some house cleaning. Drugs are something I will not tolerate."

"I know you're upset, but so far it looks like Larry and Sam were the only ones actually involved."

"I sure hope so, but whatever, I won't stop until I know every single thing that's been going on around my stables. This is my family's legacy we're talking about, not to mention my own livelihood. I'm not about to stand back and see it destroyed by a bunch of stoner dirt bags."

* * *

After saying goodbye to Gillian, Kelly got back in his truck and headed out Jacksboro Highway. *It's time somebody tracked this Sam character down.* He smacked the steering wheel for emphasis and goosed the truck. Time to pay the Texas Brothers a visit.

They had their place out in Hurst— a small community about twenty miles past Indian Creek. Kelly planned to stop at the Hideaway and pick up Jake and then head to Hurst, where if he was lucky, he might run into Ajax, one of his biker pals under his Jake persona. Probably have to leave his dog in the truck though. At the time it had seemed like a bit of fun to name the dog after his alias, but that bit of irony might just come back and bite him in the ass now that his past seemed to be crossing paths with his present.

Kelly's wife Lynda had been killed in a firebomb lobbed at his house by a drug lord. In the aftermath Kelly had quit his job as an undercover narcotics agent and moved out to a cabin at Indian Creek. He had his pension and didn't need much. Working security for the flea market paid his rent, and his needs were simple.

When a stray German shepherd had shown up at

the market one day and adopted Kelly, it had seemed like a bit of a joke to name the dog Jake. Now, however, with his past crossing paths with the present, it looked like Kelly's bit of irony in naming the dog might bite him in the ass.

* * *

"Kelly." A roar went up from inside the Hideaway as soon as Kelly pushed open the door.

"How's it going," Kelly spoke to the room at large.

Stepping inside the Hideaway was like taking a trip down memory lane. The décor—a tribute to Cam Belscher's passion for country music and country living—was a potpourri of tools and implements from the turn of the century. In a glass case behind the bar Cam proudly displayed his piece-de-resistance a cherished replica of the Budweiser Clydesdales rigged out in full harness.

Even the ceiling bore witness to Cam's passion. Glossy black and white photos of Hank Williams, Patsy Cline, Faron Young and a whole slew of long-dead country favorites smiled down on the patrons.

"How's it going?" Kelly stopped at the table where Doug Phillips and Phil Morley were engaged in a hot game of cribbage.

"Hey Kelly. Thought you went to Oregon for the wedding?"

"Got back a couple days ago. You heard about the trouble at Gillian's stable?"

"You mean that dope head that got killed over at Lake Country." Doug dropped an eight on the pile and turned to face Kelly.

"He was killed in Gillian's stable."

Doug took a drink from his beer mug and wiped his mouth on his sleeve. "Sorry to hear that Kelly. Paper said it was one of those Preston boys. To tell you the truth, we didn't pay no mind once we heard that. Those boys ain't been nuthin' but trouble since the day they were born."

"How's Bubba doing?" Phil dropped a deuce on the pile and turned his attention to the conversation.

"He's great. Same old Bubba. He sure has got a great place there in Oregon."

"Good fishing," Doug piped up.

"Oh yes. According to Bubba they've got trout in them waters bigger than catfish."

"Yeah. Well you can't take the liar out of the bait house. Sure do miss that little guy."

"Me too. It was great seeing him. You boys ought to take him up on that open invitation of his and go check out his Paradise. You won't be disappointed."

Both men nodded their heads. "Might just do that one day," Phil acknowledged the suggestion but kept on eye on Doug picking through his cards.

"Catch you boys later." Kelly strolled to the end of the bar and waited while Darlene finished serving a customer.

"Jake outside?" He asked when she joined him.

"Yep. Keeping the squirrels on their toes."

"I sure appreciate you keeping an eye on him." Kelly waved aside the beer she pulled out of the cooler and motioned to the coffee pot. "I'm heading out to Hurst so best settle for coffee."

Darlene set a mug on the counter and grabbed the coffee pot off the warmer. "How's Gillian holding up?"

"She's okay. Worried about the Stable and mad as hell at whoever's behind it all."

"I heard it had something to do with a drug deal. Is that right?"

"It appears that drugs might have been involved, but we're not sure at this point. That's part of the reason I'm heading out to Hurst. The Texas Brothers have their clubhouse out there. I'm hoping one of them might be able to give me some information about a guy named Sam."

"Sam who?"

"I don't know. He's supposed to be an old friend of Larry's brother Clinton."

"Cam booted those Preston boys out of the Hideaway the year Anna died. I haven't seen any of them since."

"They still live out here?"

"I don't think so. The old lady disowned the lot of them years ago. Last I heard she went into a nursing home and left the property to some clinic in exchange for the bill for taking care of her cat."

Kelly shook his head. "No wonder Larry was a mess."

"Do you think this Sam had something to do with Larry's death?"

"I don't know. We're pretty sure he was supplying drugs to the local school kids, but we don't know yet whether or not the murder's connected."

A series of loud barks from the back deck followed by the banging of the screen door preceded a fur covered cannonball that launched itself at Kelly and nearly tipped him off the bar stool.

"Hey there. That's some welcome, old buddy." Kelly rubbed the dog's ears and ran his hand up and down Jake's back.

"I guess that means I've been missed," Kelly said to Darlene, who stood watching the man and canine reunion and shaking her head.

"That's the most life I've seen out of him in a week. I didn't want to worry you with everything going on, but I swear this one's been pining for you for days."

Kelly finished his coffee, retrieved Jake's stuff from the shed behind the Hideaway and said thanks and goodbye to Darlene. Then, with Jake riding shotgun, he pulled out onto the highway and headed for Hurst.

* * *

Tucked away on a tree lined side street, the Clubhouse looked like any other small town residence, with the exception of the large prefab shop dominating the front of the property.

Kelly pulled into the driveway and stopped.

"Watch the truck." He rolled the window down and set Jake on guard, then walked up to the door of the shop and stopped to listen. The roar of pipes and clanking of metal on metal confirmed that someone was hard at work inside.

Pushing open the door he stepped inside and

stopped. Two men worked had their backs turned to the door and their heads bent to their work. One of them held onto a bike propped against a rack while he worked a piece of leather over a long narrow seat. The other man used a rubber mallet to bang hell out of the section of frame he had balanced over an anvil. Kelly searched his memory, came up with the name Benny and circled the bike to come up in front of the man.

"You seemed occupied so I figured I'd better make myself noticed." Kelly held out his hand. "How's it going Ben?"

At Kelly's approach the biker had stiffened and watched the intruder with narrowed eyes.

"Do I know you?"

"Jake. I know it's been a couple of years, but I figured I was more memorable than that. I'm an old friend of Ajax. I'm looking for the big guy. That's what brings me out to these parts."

"You been outta circulation, or something?"

"Let's just leave it at "or something". What about Ajax? You seen him around?"

"Not for a year. He's doing time."

"No shit. What for?"

"Not for me to say."

"Okay. Good enough. What about Gene, he still in Haltom City?"

"Far as I know."

Kelly, sensing there wasn't anything more to be learned from Ben, thanked his reluctant host and headed back to the truck. Back on the highway, he mulled over the loss of Ajax as a contact. He'd been hoping to trade on past favors, but things might not be hopeless. First he'd need to talk to Gus and see how seriously Ajax had run afoul of the authorities. Ajax had never been violent. In fact, most of his brushes with the law had been minor and easily mitigated by Miles Garrett, the bikers' lawyer of choice.

I wonder what in hell the big guy got himself involved in this time. Guess I better go find out before I waste anymore time speculating.

With that Kelly turned his attention back to maneuvering his way through the steadily building afternoon traffic and headed for Tarrant County sheriff's department headquarters on Taylor Street.

* * *

Back at Lake Country stables Gillian had called in her entire crew and had everyone assembled in the training barn.

Dressed in jeans, a red and white checked shirt, a pair of scuffed cowboy boots, with a well-worn straw covering her blond hair, Gillian stood facing four young men and one girl.

"We have several things to deal with this morning, so I'll ask you to listen to what I have to say and then, after I've covered everything there will be time for questions. We're going to be awhile, so grab a soda out of the cooler and take a seat." Gillian motioned to a large ice chest placed in front of the circle of straw bales.

After several minutes of digging through ice, selecting sodas and choosing seats on the bales, the room quieted down and all eyes focused on Gillian.

"First, most of you probably know Joel, and if you don't you can introduce yourself after we're finished." Gillian pointed to a tall, slender boy with shaggy brown hair who sat on edge of the furthest bail. "As all of you know, we've lost two of our workers. I know each of you are sad and upset about what has happened to Larry and Toby the same as I am, and there's no doubt in my mind that Detective Graham and Kelly are going to catch and punish the offenders." Gillian turned her head in a slow circle looking directly into the eyes of every one of her workers. "That being said, we still have a stable to run, and for now that's where we need to focus our attention."

Gillian paused and waited until each worker had nodded agreement, then she continued.

"First, let's deal with a very disturbing rumor that has surfaced as a result of these deaths. You may or may not know that there have been allegations of drug involvement by one or more of the members of my crew." Gillian stopped speaking and paused for emphasis.

"This is absolute." She continued. "I will not tolerate drugs in any form or by any person. If you're involved, then you might as well leave now, because you are going to be found out, and you are going to be dismissed."

Once again Gillian stopped and made eye contact with every one of the youth. Relieved, she noted that none of them flinched and no one looked away. Every pair of eyes met hers directly and held until she moved on to the next. One of them might be a master of deception, but Gillian didn't think so. Larry and Toby were dead, and whatever they'd gotten themselves into or more accurately whatever this Sam person had gotten them into, appeared not to involve the rest of her workers.

Gillian stopped for a moment, and then smiled at the young people. "We're going to need to make some adjustments to our schedule since we're still down one person. Do any of you have any suggestions?"

"I wouldn't mind switching to weekends." Mike spoke up and Gillian turned towards him.

"Oh yes, Mike, you're going to be starting your practicum this summer aren't you?"

"Yep. I'm going to be working with the police department at Tarrant County Hospital District. It's three days a week, but they need me to be flexible, so if I could move to being weekend casual here I could keep both jobs."

"What about it, Robin, are you interested in taking Mike's weekday shift?"

"I'd love it." The curly redhead with bright blue eyes and a face full of freckles squealed her excitement and Gillian smiled. Robin had asked for a full time position several months ago, but at the time there hadn't been room.

"Great. I know you've been saving for Vet school, so this should work out well for everyone."

"Does that mean Joel will be taking Toby's place?" Paul, a muscular young lad with sharp brown eyes and the kind of dark skin the sun had polished into bronze, questioned Gillian.

"Yes. Joel has spent a couple of summers

working on his uncle's cattle ranch, but he's never worked at a stable before. You won't mind showing him the ropes will you Paul?"

Paul had turned to face Joel, and apparently the two approved of what they saw in each other's eyes, because the young man turned back to Gillian and grinned. "I'll break him in good," he said, and then laughed and reached over to clap Joel on the back.

"Good. So we're going to be looking for another casual to replace Robin, but for now we should be in good shape. Anybody have any problems they need to discuss?"

Five heads shook no.

"Okay. What about the situation with Larry and Toby. Does anybody know anything they haven't mentioned?"

Paul coughed and Gillian turned back to face him.

"Toby kept a box of stuff hidden in the back of the tack room. I don't know if it's still there or not, but I figured you might want to know."

"Thanks Paul. You and I will go take a look in a few minutes. Anybody else have anything to say?"

The remaining four shook their heads, and Gillian turned to Paul. "Okay, let's you and I go check out the tack room. The rest of you," she turned to the others "can head into the house. Celestina has lunch laid out in the kitchen. Paul will join you after he and I finish in the tack room."

"Save some for me." Paul shouted after the others as they stampeded out of the barn headed for the kitchen.

* * *

After parking Old Blue in the underground, Kelly made his way to the west side entrance, cleared security and took the elevator to the 7th floor.

"Hey there Kelly. It's been a long time." The receptionist, an old friend from his days on the force, smiled and shook hands. "You here to see the big man?"

"How's it going Wallace? Still keeping them in line, I see."

"I try. I try. Hang on a minute I'll buzz Gus for you."

Wallace buzzed Gus on the intercom and no more than had time to bring Kelly up to date on the latest gossip, before Gus poked his head through the door and motioned Kelly to join him inside.

Kelly responded to several greetings called out from the cubicles as he followed Gus across the room. Now that he'd made supervisor Gus had one of the private offices. "It's open," he said, motioning Kelly inside.

"You sound like you've been having a bad day?" Kelly slid into one of the chairs fronting the scarred old wooden desk and grinned at his cranky friend.

"Media officers. As if I don't have enough going on with some lunatic running around the city killing of teenagers, I'm supposed to drop everything and go for a TV interview."

Kelly chuckled. "One of the perks of command."

Gus waved his hand in a signal to change the

subject. "So what have you got? I sure hope it's better than what we've come up with so far."

"I don't know. It depends on how you feel about turning lose one of your current inmates?"

"Who and why?"

"Ajax Barrington."

"The biker?"

"Yeah. You know Ajax?"

"We've met. I didn't realize he was inside. What for?"

"Trafficking in stolen auto parts."

Gus made a face and shook his head, then he turned to his computer, hit the keys and squinted at the screen.

"He's got eight months left. No problems, model prisoner, good candidate for early release, all the usual BS. Shouldn't be much of a problem. Why do you want him out?"

"Because I want you to turn him and put him undercover. He's a great candidate in any event. As you know the Brothers have never been into hard drugs or anything really nasty. But there have been some shifts in the power structure. The old guys are dying out and the new ones coming into the club don't have the same kind of standards."

Gus snorted. "That's a hell of a thing. Standards in a biker gang."

"You know what I mean. The lines are being blurred and a new breed is taking over. Having a guy like Ajax on the inside, someone who is part of the old guard and has a historical right to entrée into things and information can't be anything but beneficial."

"Yeah. And guys like that aren't known for cooperating with the cops, no matter what kind of private battles they're having.

"In the past that was true, but Ajax is one of the original Brothers. When I was undercover I had occasion to sit in on a couple of meetings and I know for a fact that he took a lot of pride in the Brothers being what he called a "clean" club. Of course I may have misjudged him, but my gut tells me that Ajax isn't happy about the changes being made by some of these newcomers. I think, if you approach him right, he might just consider ratting on a drug supplier to be doing a service for his Brothers."

Gus leaned back and frowned. "I'm not really opposed to this. He's inside on a minor rap and getting him out isn't the problem. I just think we need to go about it in a different way. Guys like Ajax, even if they're on board with our thinking, they just don't do business with cops."

Kelly started to speak, but Gus interrupted. "Hear me out. I'm all for giving your idea a shot, but I say we take a different approach. I'd like to set you up with a meeting on the inside. You can tell Ajax that I caught you in a minor indiscretion.

"Like what?"

"Hell, I don't know, make up something. Tell him I offered you a deal to cooperate and you took it. Tell him how you turned in a bunch of information on the Bandits."

"He'll love that."

"Exactly, as much as the Brothers hate those

bastards you should have his undivided attention."

"How am I going to translate that into a reason for Ajax to help us get Sam?"

"That's what I'm working on." Gus leaned back in his chair and Kelly waited while the Detective sorted out his story.

"You can tell him that you know the Brothers don't agree with selling shit to kids, and you need his help. Tell him I've approached you with a proposition that would catch a Yankee who preys on local kids and maybe even murdered a couple of those boys."

"I get that, but he's still going to be cooperating with the cops. I thought you said that's where he'd draw the line."

"I have a hunch it'll sit better in his craw if it's you who's dealing with the cops and he's just helping his organization get rid of a Yankee scumbag."

Kelly nodded. "You know. It might just work. Especially if I suggest this slime ball might have been brought in by one of those new members who have been trying to over-ride the old guard inside the organization. All Ajax has to do is convince his brothers that he has good reason to believe the cops are looking at Sam as a murderer. That's a hell of a lot more heat than the Brothers will want to deal with. From Ajax's standpoint turning in Sam will kill two birds with one stone. First he'll get the Yankee murderer out of the club, and even more important he'll re-establish the credibility of the Club elders and set those newcomers back on their asses. Which , if you ask me, is going to have one hell of a lot of appeal."

"That's what I figured. You tell him to say the word and you'll see that he's outside in time to sleep in his own bed."

"Sounds good. Set it up and let me know." Kelly stood and offered his hand. "I'm going back to the stables and see how Gillian's made out. She was having a council of war with the help this afternoon."

"Let me know if she comes up with anything."

"I'll give her a call. She should be done with the meeting by now."

"Sure go ahead. Want my desk?"

"No. My cell's good." Kelly pulled out his phone and touched Gillian's name on the keypad.

"Hi there." Her voice in his ear sounded excited.

"I was just getting ready to call you. I found a locked suitcase that Toby had stashed inside the tack room."

"Hang on. I'm in here with Gus. Let me put you on speaker."

Kelly pressed the sound button and set his cell down on the desk. "Okay, I've got you on speaker. Now say that again for Gus' benefit."

"After my meeting with the kids was over, I asked if any of them knew anything they needed to bring to my attention. That's when Paul told me he'd seen Sam put something into one of the lockers in the tack room a couple of weeks ago."

"What the hell?" Gus leaned forward in his chair. "Kid didn't say anything when we questioned him."

"Well, in defense of Paul, I don't suppose he figured it had anything to do with Larry's murder." Gillian defended her worker. "Remember the kids didn't know anything about Toby's death at the time you questioned them. I doubt he even thought any more about it until I asked the questions this afternoon."

"Yeah." Gus grunted.

"Did you find out what was in the locker?" Kelly steered the conversation back to the hidden object.

"Yes. It's a small black case. Looks like one of those briefcases the lawyers like to carry."

"What was inside?"

"I don't know. I left it right where I found it. I just finished sending the kids on their way. I was getting ready to call and see if you wanted me to bring the suitcase in or leave it where it was."

"Leave it." Kelly and Gus spoke in unison. "We'll be right over."

Chapter Six

Kelly turned through the gates of Lake Country Riding Academy and pulled up behind Gus' dark blue Crown Victoria.

"Took you long enough." Gus unfolded himself from behind the wheel and joined Kelly in front of the gate that led to the stables.

"Yeah. Not having that blue bubble perched on top slows me down a bit." Kelly joked as he opened the hand gate for Gus to go through and then followed his former partner down the path that led to the main barn.

"Gillian said she'd meet us inside. She's been spending all her spare time out here in the barns."

"Almost like looking after kids."

"That's the truth. She loves those horses like they were her children. Can't blame her for fussing either, what with all the turmoil that's been going on around here the past week."

Kelly led the way past the main entrance to the barn and around to a small door set into the side of the building. "This goes directly into the tack room," he said. "As you can see it would be simple to slip into and out of this side without anyone from the main buildings being aware you were even on the premises."

"That caught my eye right off." Gus followed Kelly inside and stood. "Want to call Gillian? I'd just as soon have her present before we touch those lockers."

"Sure. She should be right outside." Kelly stepped to another door, pulled it open, and called out. "You got a minute, Gilly?"

"I'll be right there." She poked her head around a stall and waved to show she'd heard them.

Moments later, brushing straw out of her hair, she joined Kelly and Gus inside the tack room. "Sorry. I didn't hear you arrive."

Dressed in faded denim with a scarf tied around her head and well-worn cowboy boots on her feet, Gillian looked like she'd been screening a spaghetti western.

"You all set?" Kelly bent to give her a quick kiss on the lips and then opened the door into the tack room.

"Hi Gus." Gillian crossed to where the detective stood waiting beside a bank of lockers. "Like I told Kelly, I bought these lockers from the school board when they built the new elementary school out at Indian Creek. I wanted a place where my workers could keep their personal stuff and these were ideal."

"So they all have their own lockers?" Gus followed Gillian down the bank of lockers and watched as she pulled a key out of her pocket and inserted it into the padlock on the far left bottom locker.

"Yes. Each of them has their own locker and their own padlock. However, this particular locker wasn't assigned to anyone. I had no idea Toby had given Sam a locker. I still don't understand it. Everyone knew that Sam was barred from hanging around the stables."

"Did Paul say how he came to know about Sam having this locker?" Kelly asked.

"Paul needed Toby's help with some bales. He knew Toby liked to hide out in the tack room. Stacking bales is hard work, and Paul didn't intend to do the work all by himself. He opened the door of the tack room just in time to see Sam closing the locker door and securing the padlock."

"Did he ask Sam what he was doing?"

"No. He says he didn't think anything about it at the time. He just asked Sam if he'd seen Toby and when Sam said he'd seen him out in the pasture, Paul took off out there. He told me he didn't give the incident with Sam any more thought until I asked them all to try and remember anything unusual they'd noticed over the past couple of weeks."

"Sounds reasonable. If you don't have any objections let's go ahead and see what we've got."

"It's all yours." Gillian stepped back and waited while Gus donned a pair of gloves before he reached inside and lifted out a black leather brief case.

"Nothing special here," Gus said, pulling a ring full of keys out of his pocket and selecting a small silver one. "Let's just see if this works." He fit the key into the lock, gave it a twist and shook his head. "Close but not yet." He took another key, tried it, with the same result and kept going. On the fifth try the key turned, clicked, and Gus lifted the lid of the case.

Inside the case held a letter sized brown envelope with PRIVATE printed on the face in bold black letter.

"Let's see what we have." Gus inserted a finger under the flap and worked it along the seam until it separated at the folds. "Photographs." He walked over to a work tables on the side of the room.

"Do you want to cover that table?" Gillian pointed to a large roll of brown paper. "I'll get it." Kelly grabbed the roll and held one end while Gillian measured out a strip the length of the table and tore it off the roll.

"Thanks." Gus turned up the envelope and poured the contents out on the table.

"What the hell?" Gus fanned the pictures out across the paper and Kelly reached over and placed an arm around Gillian's shoulders.

All of the pictures were shots of young boys. Some of the boys appeared to be as young as five or six and all of them were naked. In most of the pictures the boys had their legs spread and their privates displayed and in two of them a young boy lay on what appeared to be a fur rug, while an adult hand performed an unspeakable act.

"This is disgusting." Gillian buried her face against Kelly's chest.

"You understand, I have to ask." Gus' quiet voice belied his anger. "Do you recognize any of these children?"

"Good God. No." Gillian's voice rose in response to the horror of what they'd seen.

"I hate having to do this." Gus addressed Kelly. "But we need to know if either of you recognize any of these kids."

Kelly nodded. "We know. Just give Gilly a minute."

"Of course. Would you rather we take these to the house?"

"No." Gillian practically shrieked. "It's bad

enough knowing they're in my barn. I don't want them in my house. Let's look at them now, and then you can take them away."

It took fifteen minutes to go through all of the pictures. Twice Gillian had to ask for time out while she pulled herself together.

In his years as a cop, Kelly had seen some disgusting stuff, but the envelope full of pictures ranked right up there with the nastiest he'd ever had to handle. "I don't know what in hell we've got here," Kelly said, after they had sorted all the pictures by child and ended up with 8 piles of pictures.

"Neither do I." Gus separated each pile of pictures with a blank piece of paper, stacked them and sealed them back in the envelope. "But once I get this stuff back to HQ I can guarantee there won't be a man on the force who isn't pulling overtime until we find the perverted bastards responsible for these." Gus stuck the envelope back inside the briefcase and picked it up by the handle. "I'll take this now." He said to Gillian. "You're okay with that?"

"Yes. Please take it away from here." Gillian shuddered and her normally tanned face turned sickly pale.

"If you don't mind locking up the tack room. The CSI's already went through the place, but now they'll need to come back and concentrate on this room and those lockers specifically."

"Of course. I'll probably have to stop using this room anyhow. I'll never be able to forget those pictures.

Kelly, his arm still wrapped around Gillian's shoulders, tightened his grip and pulled her against his chest.

"Once I've taken Gillian back to the house I'll hunt up Paul and see if he has anything to add to his story."

"Good. I'll be in touch." Gus took the brief case and left.

Kelly waited while Gillian locked up the tack room so the two of them could walk back to the house together.

Jake met them part way and they both stopped to stroke the dog. Gillian bent her head to Jake, wrapped her arms around his neck and accepted his soothing licks.

"He knows we're upset." She stood and they continued walking with Jake marching between them.

"Not much gets past this old boy." Kelly's hand trailed along Jake's back as they walked. When they reached the porch Kelly led Gillian across to the awning covered swing and urged her onto the seat.

Jake stretched out alongside. A guardian watching over his adopted mistress.

"I'll get some tea." Kelly went to the kitchen, made a quick call on his cell, and returned to the porch with two ice filled glasses of amber liquid.

"I have to go back out to the barn." Gillian said, after they'd sipped their tea in silence for several minutes. "I need to finish changing the straw. Robin's going to be here soon and I need to be there. It's her first day on the new schedule and there's stuff I need to show her."

"Sure you do. It's your business. I know it's hard, but you need to put everything else out of your mind and leave it to Gus. We all suspected this Sam character was bad news, but none of us expected what we found inside that suitcase. If it's any consolation, I doubt if Toby knew about those pictures. It takes a really sick mind to deal in child pornography, and I don't think Toby had that kind of perversion in him."

"But why then? Why would Toby let Sam have one of our lockers? Why would he hold onto pictures like that? What does it mean? Where did they come from? Oh God Kelly, I feel so dirty."

"I don't know the why, and right now neither does Gus, but I'll tell you this. We're going to find out. Sam lied to Toby about what he wanted to keep in that locker."

"So how did Larry get into the picture?"

"We don't know that either, but if you want a guess, Larry was involved in Sam's drug operation. Being the nosy sort he likely overheard a conversation between Sam and Toby, or even more likely spying on Sam and catching him taking stuff out of the locker, might have stumbled onto those pictures. It could be that if we find out who and why those pictures got into your locker, we'll also find out who and why had reason to kill both Larry and Toby."

Gillian shuddered. "It's all so horrible."

"Yes it is, and that's why I want you to try and put all this stuff out of your mind. Gus is a grandfather. He loves kids, and there's nothing he hates more than a child abuser. He's going to catch the monster who's behind all this, and I'm going to do everything in my power to help.

Gillian leaned over and kissed Kelly on the lips.

"Thanks. I needed to hear that. I'll go out now and get things ready for Robin. I love you." She turned and headed for the door.

"Hey." Kelly yelled after her. "You can't just say something like that, for the very first time ever, and then take off."

Gillian stopped with her hand on the door knob, smiled and stepped outside.

Damn. That woman's really gotten under my skin.

* * *

With Gillian gone back to work, Kelly decided to do some work of his own. First he went out to the truck, gathered up the scraps of paper he'd used for scribbling his "reminders" over the past few weeks and took them into Gillian's office. Ever since his days on the force he'd been in the habit of using an evidence board to sort out details. It was the best way he knew to link up what might appear to be unimportant coincidences, but when sorted could often be seen to form a distinctive pattern.

First he cleared the surface from one of Gillian's tables, then he tore a strip off a roll of brown paper and covered the surface. Next he took a marker and started making headings.

First row **Larry's Murder**. Underneath that he jotted down: *Toby – Angelina –SAM.* Then he wrote down *Common Element.* He stood there, thinking for a long time, and then he grabbed his marker and in bold letters wrote: **PAUL KING**.

"Damn. Why didn't I think of that?"

Kelly dropped the marker on the table and turned to Gillian's file cabinet. Under "P" he found personnel, and under "K" he found Paul King. The address on his personal contacts form had him living on Camp Bowie Boulevard, a few miles from Texas Christian University--or TCU as it was usually called. Checking his watch and seeing ten to four, Kelly decided classes were likely over for the day, which meant there'd be a good chance of catching Paul at home. Kelly had some questions that he needed to ask and he didn't want to cause Gillian any unnecessary pain.

Might be a wild goose chase, but if either of those boys knew anything about that envelope they sure as hell wouldn't have let on to Gillian.

Determined to talk to Paul, Kelly headed for Camp Bowie. Fortunately it was early enough to find parking on a side street off the boulevard. A short walk took him to The Palms, an adobe style complex featuring the regulation pool in the center courtyard and loud music blaring out the open doorways of dozens of cubicle sized bachelor apartments.

Kelly followed the wall around the courtyard until he came to an unlocked wooden gate. He reached over the top, pulled the latch and walked into the pool yard. There were more than a dozen young people stretched out on poolside loungers. Several scantily clad coeds lounged around the edges of the pool, watching as athletic young males performed a variety of gymnastic maneuvers.

"Hey there." Kelly stopped in front of a group on loungers. "I'm looking for Paul King's place."

A sunburned youth with cropped hair, lifted his head and stared. "Top floor, down at the far end." Kelly must have passed some kind of test, because the boy continued. "He hasn't been out. Don't know if he's home or not. He's in number 26."

"Thanks. I'll check it out."

"Sure. No problem." The youth put his head back down on the lounger and closed his eyes.

Kelly took the stairs to the second level and walked to the far side of the complex accompanied by laughter and splashing from the pool below.

At Unit 26, he raised his hand and knocked sharply on the door.

"It's open." A muffled response came from inside.

Kelly turned the knob and pushed open the door. No shortage of A/C inside, it was kind of like stepping into an arctic cave.

"Hey. Kelly. Whatcha doing over here?" Paul sat cross-legged on a leather couch, a blanket wrapped around his shoulders and a joy stick in his hands. In front of him, on a video console, a cave monster wielding a sledge hammered away at what looked like a stack of race cars.

"Let me guess." Kelly said. "This is one of those all utilities paid buildings."

Paul blushed. "Sorry. Too cold for you?" The young man jumped up from the couch, and flicked the switch on a thermostat. Instantly the rush of blowing air stopped and Kelly settled into a chair.

"Back home in El Paso, we had eight of us living

inside four rooms, and we sure didn't have air conditioning. Guess I get a little carried away once in awhile." The kid ducked his head and offered Kelly a sheepish smile."

"Understood. I've been in a few sweat boxes myself." Kelly shifted position and stretched out his legs. "I'd like to ask you a few more questions about the incident in the tack room."

"You mean Sam getting into the lockers? I'm sorry about that Kelly. I know it looks like I was holding out on Detective Graham, but honestly I wasn't. I just didn't think about it until Gillian asked us if we'd noticed anything unusual."

"Hey. It's okay." Kelly soothed his voice to settle the lad down. "We know you weren't trying to hide anything. We just want you to go over everything you can remember about that day. Just to get our facts straight."

Paul blinked his eyes several times, and Kelly paused for a minute and then continued his questioning.

"The first thing we'd like to establish is whether or not you have any idea what Sam had in that locker?"

Paul's eyes widened and he shook his head back and forth. "I swear I never looked inside. I didn't have a key for one thing. And anyway, when I asked Toby about it, he said I'd be better off keeping my nose out of Sam and Larry's business."

"So you did mention the locker to Toby?"

Paul blushed again. "Yeah. Guess I shoulda said something."

Kelly kept his eyes fixed on the young man's face. "It would go a long way to fixing things if you settle down and tell me now, word for word, exactly what was said between you and Toby about this incident."

Paul nodded. "Okay. First of all after I ran into Sam in the tack room, I went out to the pasture looking for Toby. I found him there too, fooling around with one of the colts."

"Did you ask him about Sam having a locker?"

"Not then. I gave him shit for ducking out on stacking the bales. He made some lame excuse about checking out the colt's leg, and then we went back into the barn and stacked the bales."

"Where was Sam while this was going on?"

"I don't know. I never saw him again. Guess he left through the tack room door. Gillian didn't want him on the property so he'd make sure not to go out front where Angelina might see him."

Kelly frowned. "So even though you knew that Gillian didn't want Sam on the property you didn't tell him to leave or do anything about reporting him."

Paul shook his head. "I'm sorry Kelly. I was stupid. I just didn't want to get in between Toby and Larry and their business."

"So you know they had some kind of business going?"

"Not really. I just sort of suspected. But, hey, I was the new kid on the block. Larry and Toby are old timers. This is my first year on the regular schedule and I didn't want to screw up by rocking the boat."

Kelly nodded. "We'll talk more about that later. But let's get back to Toby. When did you have this conversation where he told you to stay out of Sam and Larry's business?"

"It was after we finished stacking the bales. We went back to the tack room to get some pop out of the cooler, and that's when I remembered. I said to Toby, 'hey, how come Sam's got a locker in here. I thought Gillian said he wasn't supposed to hang around'."

"And?"

Toby shook his head. Gave me one of those 'how'd you get so dumb?' looks and told me if I knew what was good for me I'd forget I'd ever seen Sam, and sure as hell I'd better not mention anything to Larry."

"So that's it. That's the only thing he said about the locker."

"I swear it. I never brought it up again, and until Gillian asked us about unusual incidents I completely put it out of my mind."

Kelly asked a few more questions, but he was satisfied the kid had told him everything he knew.

"I'm going to cut you a break." He said, getting up from his chair and looking down at Paul. "I'm not going to mention your failure to report these Sam incidents, but I want you to remember. If I ever hear of you even so much as failing to report a rumor about what goes on at those stables, I'll take it to Gillian and you can bet that'll be the end of your affiliation with Lake Country Stables.

"I promise Kelly. It won't ever happen again. This is the best job I ever had, and Gillian's a terrific boss. I'm sorry I was so stupid. I'll be in the office reporting it to Gillian if a stray dog so much as sneaks into the stables."

"Good. You keep your nose clean and things will work out fine."

* * *

By the time Kelly arrived back at Lake Country the sun had gone down and lights glowed from inside the house. Kelly parked and took the steps up the front porch to the main entrance. Knocking, he waited until he heard the slip, slap of sandals on the hardwood floor and the door swung open.

"You know what I'm missing?" Gillian, wearing a mint green mini dress with matching sandals, opened the door and invited him inside. Her long blonde hair, loosened from its customary pony tail, fell over her shoulders and tumbled down her back in a mass of Angelina waves.

"I'm not sure, but a man can hope." Kelly bent his head to take possession of her mouth.

"Oh yes. You can definitely hope." She murmured against his lips. "It feels like months since our last night in the cabin." She pressed against him, reveling in his instant arousal. "I'm so hot my panties are wet."

Kelly grasped her butt cheeks and pulled her tight.

"Have you any idea what you're doing to me?"

"Yep. Same thing you're doing to me. Are you hungry?"

"Damn right, but not for food." Kelly lifted her into his arms and stepped inside, gave the door a shove with his heel and headed for the staircase.

"Hurry." She whispered against his ear, spurring him to take the steps in double-time.

Inside the bedroom, Kelly stopped in front of the queen sized bed with its gleaming brass headboard and laid Gillian down on her flowery blue duvet.

"Let me," he said, bending to remove her sandals before grasping the bottom of her dress and pulling it up and over her head. "Have I told you before that you're the most beautiful woman in the world?" He bent to kiss her naval, then slid his hands inside her panties and pulled them down the length of her golden legs.

"Flattery will get you everything you want." She reached behind her head and fanned her hair across the pillow.

Kelly stripped his jeans and shorts in one smooth move and stood above her, naked and very ready for sex.

"I'll have some of that." Holding up a foil wrapped package, Gillian spread her legs and crooked her finger.

It didn't take a second invitation. Kelly removed the condom from its wrapping, slipped it on and then balancing on his arms, lowered his hips between her legs and probed her mound, prodding and pushing until her fold opened and the length of him moved up and inside pressing past her clit, deeper and deeper until he fastened the tip of his penis hard against her G-spot.

"God yes. Please harder." She wrapped her legs around his back and grasped his buttocks in a death grip.

Kelly rocked her back and forth, allowing the suction of his rock hard member to rub her spot until pleasure screamed from her lips.

Then, pulling her all the way to her pinnacle,

Kelly withdrew and pounded back inside, driving again and again, whipping them both until sweat poured off their backs and their breathing came in ragged gasps, and finally, pulling her with him, he carried them over the edge and into a mind-numbing climax.

Hours, or maybe only minutes that seemed like hours, later Gillian propped her head on her arm and looked down where Kelly lay with his dark head resting against the pillow and his lips parted in a contented smile.

"Whatever you want the answer is yes." He opened one eye.

Gillian laughed and lowered her head to press her lips against his. "Sure, make me that kind of offer after you've deadened my brain with mind-numbing sex."

"Give me ten minutes and I could be coerced into seconds."

"Tempting. But I'm afraid those horses aren't concerned about my sex life. They want their dinner."

"Speaking of dinner. How about I fix food while you tend to your slave drivers."

"Perfect. I made a salad earlier – dressing is ready to whip up. There's corn in the crisper and steaks in the meat keeper. I'll pop in for a quick shower and it's all yours."

"I suppose sharing the shower is out of the question, considering that you stressed 'quick'."

"Good guess." She turned and headed into the bathroom.

Kelly lay back on the pillows and thought about himself and Gillian. *When did all this happen?* His mind drifted back two years to that first barbecue after he'd captured Anna's killer. It's funny how easily they'd drifted together. The quiet strolls and late night visits to Bubba's bait house. The Hideaway barbecues and kick ass jam sessions. The double-dates with Cam and Stella. Somehow, without either of them making any commitments, they'd fallen into being a couple. Now, Kelly realized, he couldn't imagine life without her. *Maybe it's time to take things to the next level.*

Gillian, freshly showered and dressed in jeans and a faded *Texas Cowgirls* sweatshirt, stood in the doorway.

"You going back to sleep?"

"Nope. Got a couple calls to make, then donning my chef's hat and preparing to wow my lady."

"Great. Give me an hour and I'm all yours."

"Oh yes."

Laughing, she left the room and Kelly slid out of the bed.

Chapter Seven

In the morning Gus called to say the meet had been set for nine o'clock. Kelly grabbed a coffee to go, kissed Gillian goodbye and headed for Dallas County, where Ajax was serving his time in the Hutchins State Jail.

When his cell buzzed, Kelly touched the hands free.

"Everything's all set?" Gus' voice boomed through the speaker. "Warden's expecting you. He'll have Ajax waiting. The rest is up to you."

"What did they tell him?"

"Nothing. He hasn't a clue who or what to expect. He's just been put in a room and told to wait."

Kelly chuckled. "God only knows what kind of scenarios he'll have dreamed up in his head by the time I walk in the door."

"That's the idea. Tighten him up, get him expecting the worst, and you'll come in looking like saint and savior."

Kelly laughed. "Yeah sure. I'll report later." He pushed the button and checked the GPS, which showed another five miles to his turn off.

* * *

Kelly passed through the security gates, and followed the guard to a room with a small barred window. Inside a metal table had been bolted to the floor with two straight backed chairs set on either side. In one of the chairs, leaning forward with his elbows propped on the table, sat the biker known as Ajax.

The big man had aged since the last time Kelly had seen him. Gone was his full head of wavy brown hair. In its place a prison crew cut and evidence of a high forehead where the hair would never grow again.

"Been a long time." Kelly approached the table and held out his hand.

Ajax studied Kelly's face for several moments without raising his hand. "I'll hear you out before I return that handshake."

"Fair enough." Kelly pulled out the other chair and sat at the table. "I'm sure you've an ear to the outside so you probably know I've been asking around about you."

Ajax tilted his chair back and remained silent.

"I'd guess you've been wondering what I want so I won't keep you in suspense. I want you to help me catch a murderer."

"What the fuck?" Ajax let his chair bang down on four legs and glared at Kelly.

"Nothing to do with the Brothers." Kelly held up his hand. "Hear me out. If you don't like my proposition that's all there is to it. I'll go on about my business and you'll go back to serving your time." Kelly flattened his hands on the table. "You willing to listen?"

Ajax gave a brief nod. "I'm listening."

"Okay. First of all. The murderer isn't a local. He's a Yankee and we have reason to believe one the Brothers is helping him hide."

Kelly stopped, waited a moment, and when there

was no outburst from his listener, he continued.

"We don't think your guy knows he's helping a killer. Matter of fact, we figure this bastard has conned one of the young bucks in your organization into helping him out in exchange for an introduction to a certain West Coast drug lord."

Ajax's eyes flared, and Kelly held up his hand to stay comment. "I know the Brothers have never been into drugs, but we both know that's history. Rumor has it some of the younger Brothers are pushing for a change in leadership"

"Bull shit."

"No, it's not bull shit, and you know it isn't. But we're not interested in drug dealings and we're not after anyone inside your organization. It's like I told you, we're after a killer."

"We? You turned into a cop or something?"

Kelly shrugged. "Or something. Let's just say, the man you knew as Jake has two roles in life."

"Snitch." Ajax spat the word.

Kelly slammed his fist down on the table. "I ain't a Goddam snitch."

Ajax snorted and slid his chair back.

Kelly pulled an envelope out of his jacket pocket and put it on the table. "You've got a couple of grandkids don't you? Boys if I remember correctly."

"Yeah. So what."

"So take a look in that envelope and tell me if you want that son-of-a-bitch living in your neighborhood."

* * *

Minutes ticked by. The biker looked at the first picture, scowled, and dumped the batch onto the table.

"Are you saying the fucker who took these is staying with one of my Brothers?"

Kelly shook his head. "We don't know where he's staying. If we did he'd have been arrested. The cops have observed Sam Taylor in company with an individual known to be one of your Brothers?"

"Which one?"

"They don't know. They're not even positive of their information, it's just rumor at this point. That's why they need you – to find out whether or not there's any truth in the rumor."

"So you wouldn't be able to tell me who I'm looking for even if I did decide to go along with this."

"That's about it. We're counting on you to work from the inside – it's possible one of your guys is working a private deal. He may not realize anyone's made the connection, and he may be hiding his arrangement."

"That's not how we operate."

"That's not how the old Brotherhood operated, but we both know things are changing. Maybe there's nothing to it. If that's the case you'll have gotten yourself a free pass for nothing."

"Yeah. Thanks. Something for nothing from the cops stinks to hell and back."

"I bet it would stink a helluva lot more if that piece of shit came in contact with your grandkids?"

Ajax's eyes flared and his mouth twisted into a

nasty scowl. "I catch the bastard near them kids, it'll be the undertaker attending him not the cops."

"How do you figure you're going to make sure that isn't happening while you're locked up in here?"

"I have my ways. But let's get back on track. Say I'm willing to go along with you. Just how are we supposed to find out which Brother is hooked up with this creep? If, as you say, he's trying to undermine our organization, then it stands to reason he's keeping his association with this Sam character on the quiet."

"That's true. But the cops are betting, and I'm inclined to go along with them, that it won't take you too long to sniff out the rat."

"Okay. So exactly what's the deal?"

"Simple. As soon as I leave here and make a phone call, the wheels will be set in motion. You should be turned loose by tomorrow afternoon."

"Will I have to deal directly with the cops?"

"Nope. Your release will be handled as a standard release of a non-violent, model prisoners necessitated by overcrowding. There won't be any chance of a leak because no one will know it's anything out of the ordinary."

"And I'll get in touch with you directly if I have information to pass along?"

"That's correct. I'm giving you my cell number. By the way, my name is Kelly McWinter. No reason for you to blab that around, but if you need to get in touch with me at Central, that's who you ask for.. It's not commonly know that I'm in any way involved with the cops. Which, I'd like to keep that way. Agreed?"

"Hell yeah. No way I'm saying anything about working with a snitch."

Kelly shoved back his chair. "Let's be straightening this out right now. I told you I ain't a snitch. I used to be in the narcotic business. That's personal and it's been over for half a decade. Now I'm private, and I'm helping out a friend. I don't think helping the cops nail that perverted piece of crap is going to damage your reputation any, and it might just earn you some points that'll come in handy on down the line. Let's face it, we aren't none of us getting any younger."

"Okay." Ajax lifted his hands. "Can't say I wouldn't be on board even if it did require working one-on-one with the cops, but this is a helluva lot more to my liking."

* * *

After making sure everyone had their jobs sorted out for the day, Gillian left Mike in charge while she went to check on Angelina. The girl had been released from hospital and Mrs. Morales had called with an update the evening before. According to her mother Angelina was feeling fine and wanted to return to work. Gillian had her doubts about that, but she promised to stop by in the morning and talk with the girl.

The Morales' lived in a small frame house in Haltom City. The neighborhood had a large Mexican American community and it was evident from the array of get well cards covering the hall table that the family was well liked and being given lots of support.

"She's in the family room, if you want to go right

back." Mrs. Morales

"Thanks." Gillian smiled at Mrs. Morales and then headed down the hall to find Angelina.

"You're looking a lot better than the last time I saw you." Gillian bent to give the girl a hug.

"I'm feeling good." Angelina hugged Gillian back and her smile supported her words.

"So what's this I hear about you wanting to come back to work already?"

"Oh, please." Angelina put her finger to her lips and whispered. "You've got to let me come back to work. Mama is driving me crazy. She won't let me out of her sight for five minutes."

Gillian chuckled and lowered her voice. "She's still frightened. It was very scary for her – for all of us, but especially for your mother."

"I know, and I love her to death, but please, she's suffocating me, I really, really need to come back to work."

"Okay. Let's give it the weekend. Let you get your full strength back, and you can come back to work on Monday. Is that a deal?"

"Oh yes. Thank you so much." Angelina's face lit up in a brilliant smile. "I'm missing everyone. It's bad enough thinking about Larry, but not being able to see my friends is so hard. I've talked to Mike and Robin on the phone, but it's not the same. I need to be back there working with them. We all need each other right now."

"I understand. We'll get it worked out. I'll talk to your mom before I leave. I do have a couple more questions. Maybe now that you've had time to think about things, and you're feeling better you could help me recreate what happened that day. Between the two of us we might be able to come up with something that doesn't quite fit."

"I have thought about it—a lot. I've gone over and over things trying to remember anything that Sam or Larry might have said that could have resulted in something like this. I don't know. I didn't like Sam. There was something creepy about him, but I never thought of him as a criminal never mind a murderer."

Angelina's face crumpled and, suspecting imminent tears, Gillian squeezed her hand and spoke softly. "We know that honey. No one expected this. I saw him around the property, and like you, I didn't like him, but I certainly didn't think of anything like what happened. Are you okay? Would you rather I waited until you come back to work to ask you anymore questions?"

"No. Please, I'm okay. I want to help and I'm not going to break down. I promise. It's just every once in awhile I think about Larry and wonder if I could have done anything to stop what happened."

Gillian shook her head. "You had no way of knowing. None of us did. We all feel the same way. If we'd have known we'd have done something, but we didn't, so now we have to concentrate on helping Detective Graham and Kelly find the killer."

"Are they sure it's Sam then?"

"No, they're not sure at all. Right now they just want him for questioning. It's not just because of Larry's murder. We found something in one of the lockers – the one Larry gave to Sam."

"He gave Sam a locker. I never let him do that. Honest Gillian, I'd never have given Larry permission to let Sam keep anything at the stables."

"I know you didn't. It's one of the things about Larry that none of us knew about. Apparently Sam was giving him money. At least that's what we've figured, and it looks like Larry might have been selling drugs for him."

Angelina dropped her head. "I wanted to believe Larry when he said it was all innocent, but deep down I think I knew better. I guess he lied when he said he was going to come clean when you came back."

"Not necessarily. I do believe that Larry cared a lot for you. It's very possible that he intended to keep his word, and that could be why he was killed. Even though he lied to you about his own part in selling the drugs, he could have told the supplier that you knew and that he was getting out of the operation and that they needed to shut it down and get out before I returned from vacation."

"Do you really think so?"

"I think it's possible. Larry probably didn't realize he was dealing with killers. He probably thought if he told them you knew and he was going to come clean, that they'd skip town and you'd never find out about his involvement."

"I guess I got him killed." Angelina swiped at her eyes.

"No, you did not get him killer. His decision to get involved in an illegal drug operation probably got him killed. You cared about him, and you didn't want to see him going to prison like his brother. Obviously Larry respected you and cared about you too. He wanted to change and make a difference, but that's what happens when we choose the wrong path. We mean to make things better but too often it's too late."

"I hope what I'm telling you helps catch the killer. That way at least I'll know I helped Larry get justice."

"That's the way to think. We can't undo what's been done, but we can do everything in our power to help Gus and Kelly catch these people."

"What about the locker? Did you find anything in there?"

Gillian nodded. "There were pictures in there and they aren't very nice."

"The pictures weren't of Larry were they?"

"No. They were of several young boys. I'm afraid it's pretty ugly. The pictures make it clear that Sam was involved in child pornography."

Angelina shook her head. "Larry would never have had anything to do with that. He loved kids. He was always talking about his nephews and how he intended to see that they had a better life than he and his brothers."

Gillian nodded. "We don't think Larry was involved. In fact, we're sure none of the boys at the stable were aware that Sam was involved in anything as sick as child pornography."

"There was one thing that happened. I never thought about it at the time, but maybe it's connected."

"What's that?"

"It was the week before this happened. Sam came to the stables one day and he had this biker looking guy with him. I was in the office and I saw them making their way to the stables. I didn't like it, but I wasn't sure what to do. You weren't here and I was waiting for you to come back to see if we could ban them from coming onto the property. I should have gone ahead and done it myself, but it didn't seem like my place, and I knew you'd be back in a few days."

Gillian smiled. "You did what you thought was right. Don't second guess yourself. Do you know what Sam and this biker wanted?"

"To see Larry. I saw them go around the back towards the tack room, and I went across to see what they were up to. I was going to tell Larry to get rid of them, but they weren't talking to Larry, they were talking to Dr. Morgan."

"The vet?" Gillian frowned. "What would he have to do with the likes of Sam?"

"I don't know, but I overheard part of their conversation, and it wasn't nice. Sam was talking I didn't really listen but I heard some of it, they were talking about making videos of old guys doing young chicks, it was ugly, and they were all laughing – even the doctor. Larry showed up and they changed the subject. I didn't want to look at them anymore, and since Larry was there I went ahead and left."

"Could you tell if the doctor was part of the conversation or was he just listening?"

"I think he was just listening, but he laughed—just like the other guy. I thought they were all pigs."

"So you left them in the tack room."

"Yes. I'm sorry, that wasn't very responsible of

me. I never dreamed they were murderers or I'd never have left Larry alone with them."

"You did fine. Thank you for telling me about this incident. I'll pass it on to Kelly. I hope our vet isn't connected, but I'd like to know what they were talking about that day, and who that biker was. Did Larry seem to know him?"

"I don't think so, but I didn't stick around. Once Larry came I figured it was up to him to deal with them and I just wanted to get out of there."

"That's fine. He was probably just someone along with Sam, but I'll tell Kelly about it and he and Gus can decide if they need to follow up, or maybe they even know who it was."

"I hate all this. It's so ugly. Do you need me to look at the pictures?"

"Not the bad ones. Just a couple of shots of the boys—to see if you recognize any of them."

Angelina griped the sides of her face with her hands and squeezed. "I hope I don't. It would be too horrible."

"Okay. Take your time. I'll get them out and you tell me when you're ready to look."

"I'll just go to the bathroom, okay?"

"Of course. I'll wait for you."

"Thanks. I want to stop and make sure mama's still busy in the kitchen. I don't want her to know about any of this."

Gillian smiled encouragement. "We'll try very hard to keep her from finding out. Believe me I don't want anything like this connected with the stables. But I have to be honest with you, Angelina. If the media gets wind of this none of us are going to be safe from prying eyes and ugly speculation."

Angelina stood, her eyes bright with unshed tears. "I'll be right back." The girl slipped out of the room.

She'll be okay. Gillian observed as she watched Angelina leave. Then, resolved to finish what she'd started, she reached into her purse and removed the two photograph copies that Gus had given her to see if any of her workers recognized the boys. "God I hope not," she said aloud.

"Is everything okay?" Mrs. Morales had entered the room so silently that Gillian jumped at the sound of her voice.

"Oh. Sorry, you startled me." Gillian put her hand to her chest.

"I'm sorry. I wondered if you were finished with Angelina. Did she go somewhere?"

Gillian smiled. "She just went to the bathroom. We're nearly done. Thank you for giving us some time to talk."

The woman nodded. "I am glad. She needs to talk about what happened. She's too quiet. To me she says nothing."

Gillian rose and approached the woman. "I'm sure it's very hard on you, worrying about your daughter. She's going to be fine. It's not that she doesn't want to share with you, it's that she worries. You're her mother and she wants to protect you."

"I know." Mrs. Morales nodded. "That's why I'm glad you came. She thinks I don't know how she feels, but I do. Mothers and daughters. Some things can't be shared. Thank you for being there. Will she return to work?"

"Yes. I think so. I'll make sure she doesn't over do. I'll make her stop and take a rest in the afternoon. She'll get back to normal faster if she returns to her routine. Don't you think?"

"Yes. I am afraid, but I agree she needs to work. I'll go now, before she comes back. If you need anything you'll call me."

"That's a promise. Please don't worry. We'll take care of her."

"Thank you."

The older woman left the room and Gillian sat back down on the sofa. She placed the pictures face up on the coffee table and waited.

Minutes later Angelina returned and stood next to Gillian, bent over the table.

"I don't know them." Her voice was nothing more than a whispered sigh. "I would have hated it if I had, but I'd tell you for sure."

"I know you would. I'm glad you don't know them either. I don't really think they're from around here. No one that has been interviewed so far has any idea who the boys are, or why we're asking about them."

"Do the others know?"

"At the stable? No, I've shown them the pictures, but I haven't told them why we're looking. I'd like to keep it that way."

"I won't say a word. I hope we never have to talk about it. I know that might be impossible. If it has to come out in order to catch Larry's killer and the people making those horrible pictures, then I'll do whatever you ask."

"Good. The sooner Kelly and Gus get rid of these monsters the sooner we can all get back to our lives."

Gillian picked up the pictures, put them back in her purse and Angelina followed her to the door.

"Thank you for everything." Angelina looked up with her bright eyes, and Gillian pulled her into a quick hug.

"Of course, and thank you. Now you take care of yourself. Get lots of rest this weekend and I'll see you Monday morning."

Once back in her car, Gillian checked the time and decided that if she hurried she just might get back to Lake Country in time to catch the Vet before he finished making rounds. His routine was to stop by twice a week for a general check up and if there were any horses needing special attention, he'd discuss their ongoing care with Gillian. Normally he'd take a break about two in the afternoon and whenever she had the time, Gillian would join him for coffee in the tack room. If she hurried she might get back in time for that ritual.

* * *

As hoped, Dr. Morgan had finished in the stables and was helping himself to a cup of coffee when Gillian entered the lunch room.

"Nice to see you Ms. Gillian. I hope you have time to join me for a cup." The doctor lifted his cup in a salute and then sat down at one of the tables by the window.

"Good to see you as well Dr. Morgan. I was hoping we'd have a chance to chat." Gillian filled her cup and took the seat across the table from the Vet.

"This nasty business with Larry has upset everyone. I'm sure you've noticed that the horses are out of sorts."

"Yes." Gillian nodded. "That's why I'd like to get things back to normal as quickly as possible. You don't mind if I ask you a few questions?"

"Of course not. Matter of fact if you hadn't come down here today I was planning on calling at the house to see if you could carve out a bit of time for an old sawbones."

Gillian laughed. "I haven't heard that saying in a long time."

"A little poetic license. I believe the writer was referring to a people doctor. Still, as you know the animal members of this planet are every bit as entitled to good care as our humans."

"You won't get an argument out of me on that point." Gillian nodded to acknowledge his comment and then switched the subject. "I've heard that you had some conversations with this Sam character that the police are looking for, and I'm hoping you can tell me something about him. Angelina can't quite remember – she still hasn't completely recovered from the attack last week – but she thinks you had a conversation with him and a biker that was hanging around here."

The Vet shook his head and set his coffee cup down a little harder than necessary. "I was not having a conversation with that moron. I was making it quite clear to him and his stupid friend that veterinarians do not dispense drugs to treat an animal they've never seen."

"That's what they wanted?"

"Exactly. Just like I've told the police. Because Larry was one of your workers, and prior to this incident he had always seemed reliable, I had previously agreed to give his friend some general advice regarding a horse that was apparently suffering from an unexplained stomach problem."

"By his friend, you mean Sam?"

"That's who I thought it was, but it turned out that it wasn't for Sam at all, it was for this biker friend that he brought along." Dr. Morgan slapped the table. "This idiot didn't want advice about his horse. He wanted me to write him a prescription for Percoden, which he claimed he needed for the horse. I told him I didn't take private clients and he should get his ass to a proper veterinarian with his horse, and then I told Sam not to bother me with any more of his bullshit ideas. That was the last I saw of any of them."

Gillian frowned. "It looks like Angelina must have been mistaken. She was sure that you and the boys were discussing watching someone make a video that showed several old guys "getting it on" with young chicks. She couldn't remember the name of the place, but she thought she heard all of you discussing a nightclub where you could find a lot more of that action."

Dr. Morgan's eyes flashed. "I do not know what those young men were doing after I went back to tending the horses, but I certainly was not involved in any lurid discussion with those morons and I know nothing about a nightclub."

Dr. Morgan shook his head and huffed out a breath. "I don't mean to be unkind, but it sounds like the bump on that young woman's head has screwed up more than her memory functions."

Gillian nodded. "The doctors said it may be weeks – or never -- before her full memory returns. "But you didn't overhear any of this supposed conversation Angelina is talking about. I wouldn't keep on about it, but if we could identify the nightclub Angelina believes they were talking about it might give us a lead to Larry's killer."

"I'm afraid not. I was worried about one of the horses and I wasn't thinking about the stable boys' conversations. I don't usually listen to them anyhow. They talk the same crap all ignorant youth talk. I can't even say what they were talking about when I arrived. I didn't pay attention. All I can say is that when I was with them, they talked about horses and getting some drugs to treat some mythical horse and nothing more. Now, if you don't mind, I need to finish up here because I've several patients to see today and already I'm behind schedule."

"Of course, Dr. Morgan." Gillian stood up and offered her hand. "Please don't take offense at these questions. We all just want to clear this up and get back to our normal lives again."

"Understood. Why don't you ask this Sam some of these questions? Sounds to me like he's the one you want to be talking to."

"That's true. Unfortunately no one has been able

to find him since the murder. To tell you the truth the police think he's the killer."

"They do." The vet shook his head and rose to leave. "He's stupid enough, but I can't say I'd had pegged him as a murderer. Well, better go take another look at that Bay, she's been off her feed for a week – which, as you mentioned, could be related to all the turmoil going on around here. Let's hope it settles down soon."

The Vet left to take care of the horse and Gillian returned to the house where she sat down at her desk, took out a notepad and proceeded to write up a summary of the information she'd learned today so that she could turn it over to Kelly.

* * *

Kelly left the prison. On the highway, he called Gus.

"It's all set. Ajax is in. If you set your stuff in motion right away, he could be home by morning. Maybe we'll tie this thing up over the weekend."

"Sure as hell make my life easier. The media's having a field day – two college students dead and no suspect. It's an election year and not the kind of stuff the sheriff wants to see on the evening news."

"Of course it's all your fault."

"You got it. Can you make the White Bull for lunch?"

"My mouth's watering. See you there."

* * *

The White Bull on 28th Street had been one of Gus and Kelly's pit stops back in the days when they were a team. Kelly got a rush of memory every time he entered the brightly lit café with the 50's style décor and lip smacking aromas emanating from the kitchen. Texas favorites like chicken fried steak, biscuits and gravy, honest to God Texas chili without beans, and brisket so tender it made a knife redundant.

Inside Kelly strolled to the back of the Café, and sliding across the cracked red plastic of the same old booth he and Gus always chosen, he signaled the waitress for coffee.

"Gus'll be along in a minutes. Mind filling me up and coming back for his. You know how he likes it, hot enough to burn the lips off anyone else."

"I got you covered." Margaret had been running the lunch crowd at the White Bull for as long as Kelly could remember, and if she didn't know a person's preferences then they definitely weren't a regular.

"Like old times," Gus slid in across from Kelly and held up his cup for Margaret, who'd seen him enter and followed him down the aisle.

"The usual," she asked them both.

"Good here," Gus said, "You?"

"I'll take a bowl of that chili. Gillian's grilling tonight so better go light for lunch."

After they'd both had a couple of sips, Kelly put down his cup and brought Gus up to date on his conversation with Ajax.

"Do you think he was on the level about now

knowing who might be involved with Sam?"

"He probably didn't know then, but he'll damn well know everything within an hour of getting back on the outside. That's why I'd like to have the clubhouse staked out, as well as Texas B's. I'm not sure where he'll go first, but I'm damn certain one of those locations is a best bet."

"So will it make it better or worse that once you gave me the word I set the wheels in motion. They're processing him while we're having lunch, and if all goes as planned he'll be out before dinner."

"Plays hell with my barbecue plans." Kelly chuckled and waved his hand to indicate that he was joking. "I'll call Gillian. You want me to hang out at Texas B's? My covers good there. I'll get in on a few pool games and keep my ears open. Fred still considers himself in my debt. He knows I'm looking for Ajax -- for personal reasons. He'll give me a sign if anything starts to go down."

"Good. I'll leave a unit in the area, just in case you need backup, and take the rest out to Rhome. You get an alert you get me on my cell. We don't know what we're up against—or how many are involved. Don't take chances."

"Got you. I won't.

The men finished their lunch, and then left separately. Kelly headed for Lake Country, to explain the change in plans to Gillian, and Gus returned to the Station where he would set in motion a full scale stakeout of the Texas Brothers clubhouse in Rhome.

* * *

Kelly counted ten bikes in front of Texas B's when he pulled old Blue around back and backed the truck in alongside Fred's Marquis.

That ought to keep my fenders safe. He locked the truck and headed around to the front of the building.

Inside Bob Seger's acoustic mourned the loss of youth and self as he raced *Against the Wind.* A group of men, some Kelly recognized, some he didn't gathered around the pool table and watched Gene Robins clear the table in a single round.

"Anybody else with money to burn?" The tall hawk-faced biker lifted his head to scan the audience, and stopped when his eyes lit on Kelly.

"Jake Perkins. What the hell are you doing back in town? I thought you'd cleared out of Texas for good?"

Kelly grinned, approached the table and stuck out his hand. "Still fleecing the faithful I see."

"Fools and their money." Gene hailed the bartender. "What'll you have?" He asked, taking a seat at a booth facing the pool tables and inviting Kelly to slide in across.

"So what you been up to these past seven years? Kelly jumped in first with the questions in hopes of deflecting the attention off of himself."

"Hell you been gone that long." Gene shook his head at the idea that many years had passed.

"Seven years last month. So what's gone on with you in that time?"

"Keeping my nose clean. Got my certification five years back, been with City Electric since that time.

Donna and I made it legal after the second boy came along."

"So you've got two boys?"

"Actually we've got two boys and a girl. Little princess." Gene grinned and Kelly liked the proud papa look on his face.

"You still ride?"

"Not much. Family keeps me pretty busy. I come down here maybe once or twice a month, play some pool and touch base with the Brothers, but I'm not active anymore. What about you? Must have been something pretty drastic the way you disappeared. Wasn't the cops was it?"

"No nothing like that. Personal stuff. Lost someone who mattered. Decided I was getting too old for the lifestyle. Got an opportunity to go digging for gold and decided it was one hell of a good excuse to drop out."

"No shit. Did you find any?"

"Enough to buy myself a place off the beaten track, and not have the man breathing down my neck."

"Can't ask for more than that. Wonder what's going on over there?"

They turned towards the front door where a crowd had gathered blocking the way of a newcomer trying to enter.

"Hey give a man room." Ajax's unmistakable roar cleared the entrance as men stepped back to let the giant into the room.

The big man's eyes scanned the room, rested momentarily on Kelly, and then moved away.

"The shit'll hit the fan now." Gene commented.

"How's that?"

"You haven't been around for awhile, so you probably don't know about the unrest that's been brewing in the club. Ajax, he and Tragg and Dixie, and several of the old guard, they're trying to run the club along the same lines it's always run. It ain't lily white, mind you, but there's no hard drugs, no serious illegals, nothing more than petty shit -- hot car parts – that kind of stuff. Even that's probably gonna change after Ajax went down. I thought he had another year but they must have spring him early."

"I heard he was inside, but didn't know any details."

"Well, scuttlebutt is that someone inside the club set him up. It's a real sore spot. Touchy as hell and now that Ajax is on the outside again, things are probably going to blow wide open. There's a bunch of young blood been recruited over the past few years. They've got their own ideas about how the club should be doing business, and I can tell you, some of those ideas are going to come in over Ajax and Tragg's dead bodies."

"Tragg still the Pres?"

"Yep for now. But that's another thing. I heard rumors that a surprise election was being planned, and apparently Tragg hadn't been invited."

Kelly watched as Ajax and the small entourage that surrounded him moved to the back of the room and gathered into a tight circle.

"Whoa.," he turned back to Gene. "Sounds like a full scale revolution."

"Very damn likely. Anyway, time for me to head

back to the house. I'm getting too old for this stuff. How about you? Need a ride?"

"I'm parked out back. I figure I'd better say hi to Ajax, then I'll follow your lead. The atmosphere in here is pretty thick all right."

"Good seeing you Jake." Gene shook hands and headed for the door. Kelly sauntered over to the bar and caught Fred's eye.

"Seems a bit tense in here," Kelly observed when Fred moved down the bar to stand beside him.

"I'll be honest, Jake. I owe you one, so here's the payback. Why don't you take it in mind to head on out and get yourself a bite to eat. Nothing good on the menu here tonight."

Kelly grinned. "Thanks Fred. He reached out to shake the bartender's hand. "Nice talking to you. I'll probably be back in a day or two."

Fred nodded. "I'll look for you."

Moving quietly, keeping away from the far side of the room and the ever-growing crowd gathering around Ajax, Kelly let himself out the front door.

Back at old Blue, he pulled out his cell and pressed the button for Gus.

"Something's going down right now," Kelly said. "Fred, the barkeep I told you about gave me a warning and suggested I get the hell out of there. You might want to be heading back into town – and don't spare the sirens. I'll pull around the block and wait. Don't dawdle."

"Dawdle my ass. We'll be there in twenty."

The phone went dead and Kelly started the

engine.

He'd started to back out when the sharp crack of a gunshot had him slamming the brakes and reversing direction.

"Son-of-a-bitches better not have killed Ajax."

Chapter Eight

Inside, chaos reigned. Bikers dived for cover and Fred crouched behind the bar with a shotgun clutched in his hands. Glass from the shattered lights covered the floor. The room's only illumination came from the shadowy reflections cast by a pair of Budweiser signs hanging on the wall.

Kelly slid around the door and flattened himself against the wall, ready to drop if he spotted the shooter. Minutes passed broken only by the rustling of fidgeting bodies and the sounds of heavy breathing.

"What the hell?" He spoke to the room. "Some of you must have lighters. How 'bout striking them?" More rustling, and then the sound of Zippos flicking until dozens of tiny flames glowed and the shadows receded.

"Who's that?" Fred yelled, holding his lighter high and pointing towards a biker spread out on the floor.

"Ajax?" Kelly shouted.

"Over here." The big man called back from the far side of the room.

"Hang on, I'm getting the candles." Fred pulled a box of fat white candles stuck in bottles out from under the bar and used his lighter to get them going.

"Jake, you want to take a look?"

Kelly crossed the room and crouched beside the fallen man. "You okay?" He grasped the biker's shoulder, shook him firmly, and when he didn't get a response yanked his arm and flipped him over.

"Call the cops." He spoke aloud to Fred.

Within minutes the pounding of heavy boots broke the silence. Bikers didn't like cops, and nothing scattered them faster than hearing that the law was on its way. Kelly wandered across the room and stopped beside Ajax. "Know him?" he asked.

"Doug something. Called himself the Enforcer. Mean punk."

Kelly glanced around to make sure they weren't being watched.

"Think he might be our guy?"

"Wouldn't surprise me. I need to get out of here."

"No you stick. If they pull you in I'll take care of it. I need to get out of here before they arrive, one of them might recognize me from the meetings I've been having with Detective Graham. I don't want to get tagged. As far as they know you're a newly released inmate stopping in the bar for a couple of cold ones. As soon as I'm loose I'll get in touch with Gus and let him know you're on site. He'll see that you're not held. Now go square things with Fred. Tell him you're going to stick around to talk to the cops. He'll appreciate that."

"Shit."

"Keep your eyes and ears open. This guy could be the one we're after or this whole thing could be completely unrelated."

Ajax started across the room and Kelly slid out the back door. The last thing he needed was one of his former cop buddies recognizing him and outing his identity.

Back in his truck Kelly squealed out of the parking lot, signaled the patrol car Gus had posted down the block and headed up Belknap. After putting a couple miles between Old Blue and the bar, he pulled over to the curb and took out his cell phone.

"All hell's broken loose at Texas B's" he said, when Gus answered the call.

"Yeah. Heard it on the scanner. Johnson let me know you'd cleared out. I told him to hang back until we get there. We're headed into town now. Looks like you picked the right target."

"Not sure if the dead guy's the one we're looking for—could be a coincidence. Ajax identified him as some punk who called himself 'the Enforcer'."

"So where's Ajax now?"

"He's at the bar. I told him to stay around until you got there and you'd see he wasn't held."

"You sure he wasn't the shooter?"

"Nope. He was on the far side of the room surrounded by a group of his brothers. Fred said the shooter entered through the front door. I'd no sooner pocketed my cell from talking to you when I heard the shots come from inside. Naturally I thought someone had put a hit on Ajax, but when I got inside and had Fred put some light on the situation, Ajax and his brothers were down on the floor over in the same spot I left them."

"Did you see anyone on your way inside?"

"Nobody. Whoever the shooter was, he knew the bar well enough to know that there was a hidden door behind the men's room. It leads to a patch that takes you into a wooded area out back and allows you to cut right through to the next block. Of course the bikers use it to duck out of the place anytime the cops happen to show up, but if you aren't part of the inner circle you'd never know that door was there. It's well hidden, and it's not common knowledge."

"Which makes it more than likely that the shooter was known to some or all of those present."

"Maybe, but Fred claimed not to recognize him, and I don't think he was lying. I kind of like the possibility that the shooter might be Sam. If the dead biker was an associate, like we've been thinking, and Sam decided it was getting too hot around Fort Worth and he wanted to tie up loose ends before he left for greener pastures, shooting his accomplice in a bar full of the guy's biker buddies, would give the cops plenty of suspects. It's not unlikely the dead biker mentioned that side door to Sam thinking it might come in handy at some time or other."

"Possible. So what's next on your agenda?"

"As soon as you set Ajax loose I'm going to hook up with him for a little heart to heart. If this Enforcer character is our link to Sam, then somebody in that brotherhood is bound to know something and I need Ajax to find out who and what."

"Okay. I'll turn him loose as soon as he gives his statement. Where you headed?"

"Back to the ranch. I'll check in with Gillian. When you spring Ajax tell him to give me a call on my cell. I'll be waiting."

* * *

At the ranch, Kelly stopped on the porch to spend a few minutes with Jake, who had dashed in from the stables when Old Blue pulled into the drive.

"Miss me boy?" Kelly wrapped his arms around the big shepherd and rubbed his ears in welcome.

Jake replied with a couple of sharp barks and after a few quick licks of Kelly's hands, he bounded down the stairs and back out to the stables.

So much for who's missing who, Kelly chuckled.

Inside he tossed his jacket on the rack and stood his boots in the corner, then padded, sock feet, into the sitting room Gillian used for her office.

Bent over her laptop, she typed with concentration.

Kelly approached, stood behind her for a moment, and then touched her shoulder.

"What—?" she jumped back positioning her feet for flight or fight.

"Whoa." Kelly threw up his hands and laughed. "Good thing you're not packing a weapon."

Laughter crinkled Gillian's eyes, and she reached out to draw him into a hug. "Sorry, I was concentrating so hard on remembering everything I'd heard today I forgot where I was."

"So that's your report?" Kelly indicated the page open on her screen.

"Yep. I know how meticulous you are about recording every detail, and I thought it would be a lot easier for you to follow if I put everything down while it was still fresh so you could read it yourself."

Kelly tilted her chin and bent his lips to hers. "You are one smart woman," he murmured against her lips. "Once we're done with all this we need to focus on what a guy does when he's got the smartest woman in Texas wrapped up in his arms."

Gillian's sharp intake of breath and sparkling eyes hinted at an emotion she quickly tamped down. "I like the sounds of that," she whispered.

"Now let's see what you've got here." Kelly took her place at the desk, and Gillian stood behind with her arms resting on his shoulders.

He read for several minutes and then turned to face Gillian. "So Angelina didn't know anything about that locker, which is just what you said and both Gus and I suspected."

"I'd have been devastated if she did." Gillian brushed her hand across her eyes. "Lately I've been second-guessing everything, including my relationship with all of my staff, but I don't know if I could have stood to find out I was wrong about Angelina."

"You were exactly right. Everything you've written here rings true to the type of person you've conveyed Angelina to be, and I'm sure Gus will agree that she is not suspected of any kind of involvement in whatever scheme this turns out to be."

"Thanks." Gillian rested her forehead against his. "That means a lot."

Turning back to the screen, Kelly read the notes on her conversation with Dr. Morgan and his version of events in the stable.

"I have to say the doctor sounds a lot more credible than either of those kids."

"I know. He didn't seem evasive to me – more annoyed at those boys for trying to pull the wool over his eyes about the drugs."

"The only person I know who might know something about the nightclub that Angelina overheard the boys talking about is Mike."

"Mike. But he wasn't even working that day."

"I know that, but as you're probably aware Mike fancies himself a bit of a detective. He seems to know an awful lot about what goes on around here, and I'm thinking that might not be just from casual observation. I wouldn't be at all surprised to discover that he spent a portion of his spare time spying on his employer and his co-workers."

"His employer. Me. Are you saying Mike's been spying on me?"

"I wouldn't be surprised. But don't get all upset. I'm sure there's nothing sinister in his intentions. He's majoring in criminology, right?"

"Yes. But he's supposed to be focusing on forensics."

"Still and all, there are other components to the curriculum. I know, I've taken it myself. Hands on observation can be very valuable in developing a thesis. A place like this would be fertile ground for an active mind like Mike's."

"Well he'll be getting a very fertile piece of my mind when this is all said and done with."

"Steady Tiger." Kelly reached around and pulled her into his lap. "Got a couple hours?" He asked lifting his eyebrows and doing his best imitation of a lecher.

"Funny you should mention that." She twisted around to face him. I was just thinking I needed to go upstairs and change the linens in the bedroom. Want to help?"

"I'm your man." Kelly lifted her off his lap and took her hand. "Lead on," he said, at the very same moment as the *Battle Hymn of the Republic* rang out of his pocket.

"Damn." He pulled out his cell and flipped open the cover silencing the melody. "Ajax. When did they turn you loose?" He listened while Ajax filled him in on the events at the bar following Kelly's departure. "Okay," Kelly said into the phone, "I'll be there in fifteen." Flipping it shut and turning to Gillian, he lifted both hands in a gesture of hopelessness.

"I know, she cupped his face with her hand. That's your biker contact and you have to meet him now. I'll take a rain check."

Kelly pulled her into his arms and held her butt pressed against the front of his jeans until that familiar feeling had them both squirming for more.

"I will be back." He stepped away and pressed down the bulge in his pants. "And that's a promise."

* * *

Ajax had named a country western place on Belknap named *Sandra Kay's* and Kelly mentally approved the choice. It was a neighborhood bar with a regular blue collar clientele where they were unlikely to come across anyone either of them knew.

After standing inside the doorway scanning the

few occupied tables, Kelly spotted Ajax in a booth back by the pool tables.

A customer and a bar maid worked the sticks, fighting over their shots and laughing good naturedly. When Kelly slid into the seat across from Ajax, the girl stopped playing to ask his pleasure then quickly returned with a longneck.

"Thanks." He handed over a bill, and motioned her to keep the change.

"Good choice." Kelly said, turning to Ajax. "You have any trouble back there?"

"No, none. Kept forgetting you were Kelly and not Jake. Hell of a note when a man names himself after his dog, or visa versa."

Kelly laughed. "Yeah. Life was a bit more complicated back then. So, down to business. What went down after I left?"

"About what you'd expect. The place cleared out pretty damn fast, but a few of the boys stuck around. Street patrol burst in there like storm troopers. Lined us all up against the wall and played the bad boy bullshit."

"Rookies." Kelly shook his head.

"Snot nosed kid practically took his badge out and spit shined it on the spot. We let him spout his shit, and stood back against the wall and kept our mouths shut."

"Productive."

"Yeah. But then Detective Graham showed up. Decent cop – if there is such a thing – he rousted the rookies back out to the street and took over. We told him what we knew, which wasn't a hell of a lot."

"Anybody make a positive ID?"

"Stan went to school with the guy. His name was Doug Gillespie. He's one of the new breed of assholes they've been letting in the club the past couple of years."

"So he was a member of the Brothers?"

"Not full. He was a probie, and if he hadn't ended up dead, he'd have been booted as soon as I got out and back in charge."

"Did you ask around about Sam?"

"Not yet. Didn't have time. We're having a meeting tonight at midnight. Everyone's been ordered to show. If there's anything to find out I'll get it then."

"Good. I sure hope you come up with something. I got another question. You ever hear of a nightclub, or bar, or an after hours club of some kind, where someone with the right credentials can get access to girls who are not strictly legal?"

"What the hell you take me for? I don't mess around with babies."

"I know that Ajax. I just need some help here. You may be pure as the driven snow but seems to me there's been more Brothers with horns than wings anytime I've been around." Kelly grinned and Ajax scowled. "All I'm asking is that you put out some feelers. See if anyone knows of such a place. They're a hell of a lot likelier to share that information with a biker dude like yourself than a suspicious stranger like I've become or worse yet, a cop like Gus."

"I'll see what I can find out. Son of a bitch. I don't like any of this shit at all. I just hope you nail that pervert's ass, put him away for good and we can get back to doing our own kind of business."

"Amen." Kelly held out his hand, received a shake in return, and both men left the bar.

There wasn't much point in going back to the ranch this early. Gillian would be busy with chores and his presence would just serve as a reminder to all the kids of Larry and Toby. Right now they needed some space. Gillian needed to settle everyone into their new routines and they all needed to get their jobs done. Kelly sat in the truck for awhile, thinking about the case, and wondering where he might find his next lead, when he remembered Buddy Thorpe.

Now why in hell didn't I think of Buddy right off? Kelly spoke his thoughts. There isn't a topless club in Fort Worth where he doesn't own a piece of the action, or know who does.

With that, Kelly pulled out of Sandra Kay's parking lot and merged into traffic on Belknap. *This seems like the perfect time to collect on that chip Buddy told me would be good any time I ever needed a favor.* Kelly headed back towards downtown Fort Worth.

* * *

Pulling into the nearly empty parking lot of a long square building, Kelly found a spot around the side and parked Old Blue. The exterior of *Tickle Me Pink* had been painted black with a wide pink ribbon wrapped around the bottom and tied into a bow at the doorway. It was clever in a gaudy sex club kind of way.

A flashing neon sign on the roof spelled out *Tickle Me Pink* in pink neon with Buddy's logo "Girls,

Girls, Girls" flashing on and off in neon white. The bold neon against the flat black made quite an impact, and just to make sure nobody missed the nature of the club, covering the walls on either side of the entrance were half a dozen life sized posters of nearly nude girls wearing pink pasties and g-strings.

The dark interior of the club kept patrons' eyes focused on the stage in the center of the room. At the moment a skinny black girl in a red halter and shorts was sliding up and down a pole while two old guys nursed mugs of beer and watched the girl with avaricious eyes.

Across the room, behind a small leather padded circular bar, a bored looking bartender leaned on the counter.

"What'll you have?" she asked, when Kelly approached.

"I'm looking for Buddy. You want to tell him Kelly McWinter would like a word."

The girl raised her eyebrows and pursed her lips. "I'll see if he's here."

"Unless the evangelicals have converted him, and I don't see no signs of that in here, Buddy's never anywhere else until at least noon."

That got a giggle and a toss of her bleached blonde head. "You wait here. I'll be right back." She pulled a key out of her pocket, locked the till and passed through a curtain behind the bar.

Kelly pulled out a chair at one of the tables beside the bar and turned to watch as the music escalated in volume and the girl on stage twisted and gyrated her body into a series of uncomfortable looking contortions. Finally, on a clashing of cymbals, she reached behind and pulled away the halter while simultaneously bending forward to allow an extra large pair of silicone enhanced breasts fall forward almost into the faces of the two old men who simultaneously smacked their lips and reached forward with dollar bills clasped in their hands.

"Nice jugs." The three hundred pound club owner squeezed himself into a chair on the other side of the table. Kelly turned to Buddy and watched while he set a wine glass on the table and grinned at Kelly. "Something tells me you're here for more than the scenery."

"You always did have good taste." Kelly smiled and stuck out his hand. "Nothing at all wrong with the scenery, but you're right, it's not what brought me around today."

The big man wearing a white shirt with rolled up sleeves produced a hand sparkling with gold and diamond rings and returned Kelly's shake. "What's it been 6 or 7 years? I heard you left the force."

Kelly nodded. "Yes, I've been doing private work for a few years now."

"Good to know. Got a card?"

"Of course." Kelly smiled and produced one of his PI cards. "I'm helping Gus on a matter and I've come across something that crosses into your area of expertise."

Buddy opened his eyes wider and let out a bark of laughter. "My area of expertise, I like that. I wonder what it is the cops are wanting to know about the booby business?"

"Unfortunately there isn't anything funny about

the stuff we've come across."

"Not involving any of my clubs I hope."

"No nothing like that. It's your knowledge I need. As a matter of fact, it's something along the lines of that matter you and I got involved in way back when, but this one isn't innocent like that was. This time we're talking about deliberate child endangerment, and it may even be connected to murder."

Buddy started shaking his head when Kelly mentioned child endangerment and the look on his face had turned stony.

"You won't find one single girl in any of my clubs that hasn't got 100% straight up over 21 identification. I owe you for that wakeup call because I damn well learned my lesson. If it hadn't been for you I could have lost the whole damn works and ended up with a record that would have kept me out of the business for good. Nobody fools me with fake anymore."

"If I hadn't believed you'd been conned at the time I wouldn't have handled it like I did. This time, I'm simply needing to trade on your knowledge and experience in the business."

"What is it you want to know?"

"The name of any club or clubs that you have any suspicion might be willing to bend the rules in regard to underage dancers. And more specifically, do you know of any clubs that might be offering more than dancing to their customers? The outfit I'm looking for would features foreign girls, particularly Asians. They'd have a legitimate club, of course, with legal age girls performing, to keep from arousing suspicion, but what

I'm looking for is a club that has an after hours, by invitation only, operation catering to specific clientele and offering an entirely different group of girls from the ones most of the members see when they come in to watch the performances."

"Damn Kelly. You're putting me in a spot here. Like I said, I keep my nose clean and my girls cleaner. We're not into anything even slightly on the shady side. But, that's not to say some of my competitors aren't, shall we say, a bit more liberal minded than Thorpe Enterprises. Sure, I hear stuff, but nobody's going to appreciate me sending the cops around snooping into their business."

"I get that. And, unless there's no choice in the matter, like the cops needing your testimony to bring a murderer to justice, nobody is going to know the source of my information." Kelly tilted his head and locked eyes with Buddy. "I wouldn't be spending a chip like the one I have from you if the favor wasn't on the dicey side, now would I?"

Buddy sighed and spread his hands out on the table. "Guess you got me there. Okay, if I was a betting man – which is not something I'm sharing with any cops," Buddy grinned, "I'd be 99% certain that you'll find what you're looking for if you check into a place named *The White Turtle Club*."

"That's it? Nobody else comes to mind?"

"You asked for my opinion, and that's what you got. If I was you I wouldn't waste time looking at any of the others."

"That's good enough for me." Kelly stood up but

Buddy held up his hand. "Hang on a minute you're going to need a card. Ginger, bring me that box where I keep my passes."

The bartender took a square black box off the shelf and brought it over to Buddy, who reached into his pocket, took out a small silver key, inserted it into the lock and opened the lid. "Here you go," he said, after sifting through a stack of cards and removing a pink plastic card covered with silver print.

Kelly took the card and held it in front of the candle burning in the center of their table. "*The White Turtle Club*" he read, "That's out Highway 287."

"That's right. It's a private membership club. You'll need the card to get you inside. Of course you understand that those cards are privately issued, so the owners are going to know where you got your invitation."

"I get it, and I'm grateful Buddy. I know this puts you on the spot. I wouldn't ask if I wasn't about as sure of my conclusions as you are that this is the right club."

Buddy nodded. "There's no use in your going over there until at least one in the morning. There won't be any of the kind of action you're looking for until the regular crowd has gone home for the night."

"Got you, and thanks." He offered his hand again.

"You're welcome," Buddy returned the handshake. "Once you've finished with this business I wouldn't mind knowing what it's all about. Maybe we can combine business with pleasure and take on a couple of platters of ribs over at Angelo's."

"Makes me hungry just thinking about that

barbecue." Kelly smacked his lips. "You can consider that a promise. As soon as the cops have finished their work and everything's out in the air I'll call your girl and set up a date and time."

Before pulling out of *Tickle Me Pink's* parking lot, Kelly took out his cell phone and called Gillian. "What do you say to my stopping by Luigi's and picking up dinner for two?"

"I'd say you will be entitled to a huge reward. Especially if that dinner includes a bottle of Chianti."

"The lady's wish is my command. I'll be there in half an hour."

Ten minutes later Kelly stopped at Luigi's Deli on Forest Park, selected two orders of cannelloni with Italian sausages, a bottle of Chianti Classico and a loaf of freshly baked Italian bread. He'd have to leave for *Tickle Me Pink* about midnight, but there'd still be a couple of hours to kill after dinner and considering how scarce personal time had been for the couple, Kelly figured they wouldn't have any problem figuring out what to do with themselves until it was time for him to leave.

Chapter Nine

"That was wonderful." Gillian wiped her mouth with her napkin and picked up her wine glass. "I'm so full it's a good thing I'm not wearing my jeans because I'd probably have to unzip them."

Across the table Kelly placed his fork down on his plate, and lifted his wineglass to hers. "Got any ideas on how we might work off some of that pasta before we both have to consider new wardrobes?"

Gillian stood and reached for Kelly's hand. "Why don't we take these wine glasses upstairs and I'll see if I can think of anything."

In the bedroom, Gillian stripped off the simple cotton dress she'd been wearing and laid it, together with her bra and panties, on the stand beside her queen sized bed and lay down on her back.

"An invitation not to be refused." Kelly dropped his jeans and briefs on the floor and slid onto the bed. Leaning over, his eyes took in her golden hair fanned out across the pillow, her blue eyes smiling into his and her slim golden limbs, with perfectly formed un-siliconed breasts and warm pink nipples standing stiff with arousal. "Delicious." He bent his head and fastened his lips over one nipple while he gripped the other and gently kneaded it between his fingers.

"I'm so ready for you." Gillian opened her legs and Kelly moved between them until his manhood probed her mound. "And I for you," he breathed, entering and filling her.

"Oh yes." She wrapped her legs around his back and tightened her muscles as she joined him in the universal dance of love.

* * *

It had taken every ounce of will power Kelly possessed to drag himself out of Gillian's queen sized bed and into the night, to visit the kind of bar that didn't now and never had held the slightest interest for him.

In the first place, he liked his women wholesome and healthy, something you seldom found in the dim environs of shady nightclubs, and in the second place, he was definitely not partial to silicone. The old adage that any more than a mouthful was a waste might be a crude way to describe his preference for compact healthy female breasts, but the description, tasteless as it might be, was apt enough and one he'd definitely make sure Gillian never heard come out of his mouth.

The White Turtle turned out to be an old Southern mansion set way back from the road at the end of a tree lined drive. The mansion had obviously been restored to its former glory and judging by the brilliant glow lighting the mansion and all the surrounding outbuildings and gardens, it sure fit the profile of a private membership club. *Real cozy,* Kelly thought. *If we're on the right track then sure as hell the upper story of this place has been converted into private bedrooms.*

Taking out his cell phone, Kelly got Gus on the line. "This place sure fits the bill for one of those private membership clubs. It's just past the Radium Road turnoff of Highway 287. It's secluded and sits well back from the road. There's a gate, where I'll probably have to show the card Buddy gave me. No sign of any other security, but they wouldn't make that obvious in any case. If the operation is anywhere near as complex as you think it might be, then they'll probably have plenty of muscle inside and out of sight.

"Okay, I know the area. There's a side road just beyond you, we'll get prepared for a raid whenever you say the word. Just press speed dial on your cell and that's be our signal. Make sure you don't hit it by mistake, because once I get your call we'll light that place up like the fourth of July."

"Good. I'm going in now."

Kelly hung up the phone and pulled up to the gate, stopped his truck and rolled down his window.

"Do you have a membership card?" A metallic voice came over a loudspeaker.

"I'm a guest of Buddy Thorpe. I have one of his cards for introduction."

"Drive through and around to the right side of the building. You can park there and someone will meet you at the door on that side.

The gate opened and Kelly drove through the gates and down the long driveway. There were about a dozen cars in the front lot, not full by any means, but Kelly followed instructions and pulled around to the right side of the building.

An unobtrusive door near the back of the building stood open wide enough for the head and shoulders of a small Asian woman, who waved at Kelly when he got out of the truck and signaled for him to come down to that door.

The woman asked for his card, took it to a computer, entered what Kelly presumed was the number printed on the back of the card, and returned the card to Kelly.

"Follow me. Someone will come and get you shortly. Do you care for a refreshment?"

"Nothing right now. Thanks." Kelly smiled and the girl opened a door and motioned for him to enter.

Inside Asian screens had been strategically placed to shield patrons from the direct gaze of each other. The room was heavily draped with red and gold wall hangings and a humidor sat beside each overstuffed chair. Cigar smoke and something else – opium maybe – hung in the air.

Kelly followed the Asian girl to a chair and sat. Kelly had seen the outline of at least two other patrons, but nobody spoke. Minutes passed, and Kelly thought about his next move.

He didn't want to signal Gus until he had positive proof of what the operation was selling. He needed a cover story, good enough to get him accepted as a customer, but not so good that he'd find himself having to take a girl into a room himself. In order to make a solid case for child endangerment and juvenile prostitution, Gus needed the testimony of a patron who actually had sex with one of those kids.

Of course that meant that the patron was going to have to be given immunity in exchange for his testimony, and that stuck in Kelly's craw. He'd been around long enough, though, to know that sometimes you had to throw some of the little ones back if you wanted to nail the big ones. They didn't really know if this club had any connection to the pictures found in Sam's locker, but it was a reasonable assumption that if the owners were involved in juvenile prostitution they wouldn't turn their noses up at the extremely lucrative child pornography market.

Involuntarily Kelly clenched his fists – those girls were the real victims, but right now he needed to keep his focus. He wasn't sure what, if anything, he'd be able to find out about Sam and his connection to this place, but for now he'd be satisfied just finding out how the operation worked. Once he had observed and could testify that the club was running an underage prostitution ring under the guise of a membership club, Gus could come down on them hard, and any connection Sam had with the organization would become a bargaining chip between the beleaguered owners and their lawyers, with Sam most certainly coming out the loser.

Of course this could all be a big coincidence. Angelina could have misinterpreted the conversation she'd overheard, or dazed from the concussion she might be putting together snatches of things she'd heard from different people and at different times. Concussions were known to scramble brains, so it wouldn't be out of the realm of possibility that her memory had patched together a whole series of unrelated statements into what seemed like the same conversation.

Kelly yawned and stretched out his legs. Tough climbing out of that bed and having to sit in this overly warm room and keep himself awake.

Keep your mind on the matter at hand. He forced his thoughts away from Gillian and the bed and back to what he'd read in Angelina's statement.

Certainly Dr. Martin seemed to be innocent of any involvement. That didn't mean that Sam and one or two of the other boys weren't having a conversation about underage girls and a club where you could get special treatment, after the doctor left them, and when Angelina overheard their conversation she just assumed the doctor was still there because he'd been with the boys when she saw them talking together earlier.

Getting up and crossing the room, on the pretense of looking for a bathroom, Kelly stuck his head through the door and an Asian girl padded over to inquire.

"Wait not much longer." She reassured him. Kelly smiled and spoke in a lowered voice.

"I'd appreciate a men's room."

"Oh. Is back inside. The door by the window." She pointed towards the left, and Kelly nodded and stepped back through the doorway.

Under the guise of looking for the door the girl had indicated, Kelly managed to get a glimpse of the other two customers in the room. One, a middle aged Chinese businessman in his 40s and the other an elder statesman type with steel grey hair and one of those waxed mustaches popular in the 1930s.

To keep his inquiry legitimate, Kelly crossed to the door in question, entered, waited a few moments, flushed the toilet and washed his hands. When he returned to the sitting room the Chinese business man was gone.

I better come up with something plausible in a hurry. Kelly needed an explanation for his presence that would allow him to ask questions – and get a look at what was on offer inside – without actually putting himself into a room with an underage girl.

A different girl entered the room and escorted the old guy through a back door.

Guess I'm next. While sitting there pondering the situation Kelly had come up with what he hoped was a workable plan. Things seemed to be moving faster now, so he'd likely get a chance to test his idea very soon.

That proved to be exactly the case when a couple of minutes later the girl who had taken the elder statesman away came back through the same door and approached Kelly.

"My name is Mia." She held out her hand.

"Kelly McWinter. Nice to meet you ma'am."

"You are a guest of Mr. Thorpe, yes?"

"That's right little lady." Kelly turned up the wattage on his smile and thickened his Southern drawl. "Buddy 'n me go way back, and when I went to see him with a little problem he suggested this place."

"Ahhh, I see," the girl gave him a knowing smile. "Gentlemen with problems often find us very helpful." She'd jumped to the conclusion that Kelly was suffering from impotency, just as he'd hoped she would. Now to work that angle. If he could convince her that he'd been having fantasies about an older man making it with an Asian school girl, and that fantasy was the only thing that gave him any sexual release.

"You follow, yes?" The girl stopped in front of a *Gone with the Wind* style staircase and indicated that

Kelly should follow her up.

As he climbed, Kelly went over his story. It was going to be tricky getting permission to watch another girl with one of their customers. Undoubtedly their members had an expectation of privacy, but Kelly had come prepared to pay for any little favors he might be able to wheedle out of the staff. It was worth a try. If that didn't work, he'd have to settle for accepting a school girl – he'd hold out for that to make sure they gave him one of the young ones. When he got her into the room, if she spoke any English he might try to explain, but if not, he'd make the call to Gus and hang onto the girl at all costs. His testimony wouldn't be as good as that of a patron who had actually used the girl, but it would be better than no testimony at all, and with luck they might get the girl to name some of the men.

* * *

"You wait," the girl held open the door of a *Victorian* era sitting room.

Kelly tentatively sat down in the fancy looking, heavily carved chair that sat in front of the ladies writing desk, and waited. A door on the side of the room opened and a woman of indecipherable age entered. She had her face painted that ghostly white favored by Oriental opera stars, and her jet black hair fastened high in a double bun and lodged with two carved wooden hair sticks.

The woman took at seat behind the desk and sought Kelly's eyes.

Shifting straight in his chair, Kelly met her stare.

"Howdy ma'am," he drawled "I guess you must be my hostess."

The woman nodded, still unsmiling and opened a folder that had been placed on the desk.

"You seek a companion?"

"Well, uhm, yes ma'am," Kelly blushed and dropped his eyes. "You see, I've uh, got this little problem."

"Yes."

"It's embarrassing, but I guess you've heard it all before."

The woman bobbed her head up and down and waited for him to continue.

"It's the dangdest thing. I can't seem to get anything done when I'm with a woman. I've tried lots, and every time it's the same thing. We get it going, I'm in the preliminaries, she's ready and prime, and as soon as I go to drop my pants little Willie shrivels up like a boiled peanut. The only thing that gets me hard enough to give myself a wank is looking at pictures of old guys getting it on with school girls." Kelly coughed and tried to smile, but the woman stayed stone faced, and Kelly cut the smile.

"You want a school girl?"

"No, well, yes, maybe, but what I really want is to watch the same kind of action that I've been seeing in the pictures, and then, if it gets hard, I'd like to maybe join the couple and see if that might work."

The woman shook her head. "Our customers demand strict privacy."

"Yes ma'am. I respect that. Like I said, I know this is unusual, but I've come prepared." Kelly reached into his pocket and pulled out a thick wad of bills, with hundreds showing on both sides. "Perhaps you could talk to one of your customers?" He held out the money.

"I'll see. Wait here." She grabbed the bills and left the room.

I figured them Franklin's would get miz frigid face moving. Kelly chuckled silently.

About ten or fifteen minutes had passed when the woman stepped back into the room.

"Come with me."

Kelly stood up and followed her down the hall, up a flight of stairs and down another long hallway. She stopped in front of a red padded door and turned to Kelly.

"Inside you will sit in front of the window and watch. No speaking, while there is filming. After, I'll come back inside and if you like, we will discuss the next part of the arrangement.

She's got a taste of the money and figures there's more where that came from. Kelly calculated.

"About the film," he motioned towards the camera aimed at the window. "Will it be available?"

"We will discuss after."

Ahh, another dip in the wallet. Won't she just love it when Gus grabs up all these goodies.

Kelly nodded and took his seat in front of what he assumed was a one way mirror.

"Remember, no noise." The woman pointed at his crotch, and Kelly gave her a sheepish grin.

A sloppily fat man in his late fifties or early sixties, wearing a red velvet dressing gown entered the room, dropped the robe, and spread eagled on the bed.

Gross. Kelly shuddered.

A minute later the door opened and a dainty little Asian girl entered the room. Dressed in a tiny bra and even tinier bikini panties, she looked to be about twelve.

The girl approached the man on the bed and stopped. He lifted a finger and motion her forward.

Kelly stiffened and reached for the cell in his pocket.

Inside the room the girl stepped forward and lard ass grabbed the front of her bra and yanked it of. Instinctively the girl covered her breast, and the bastard slapped her hands away.

"Son-of-a-bitch." Kelly pressed the button that would bring Gus and his entourage.

Turning back to the window, Kelly stifled an urge to dive through and rescue the girl. The man had both arms wrapped around her waist and appeared to be struggling to lift her onto the bed.

Stupid bastard. She wouldn't weigh more than 90 pounds soaking wet. Desperate to stop what was going on in the next room, Kelly grabbed the film out of the projector, and shoved open the door. To hell with this shit. Gus would have to get enough off this tape to make his case or break the asshole in the room. No way Kelly was letting that sick pervert go any further with that kid.

* * *

Hours later, after giving instructions to his team regarding the parties rounded up in the raid on the house, Gus joined Kelly in the front seat of Old Blue.

"How you holding up?"

Kelly shook his head. "There isn't much I haven't seen or had to handle, but that one got me. I tried to get as much as I could on tape, but no way in hell could I sit back and let the monster take that little girl."

Gus nodded. "I appreciate that Kelly. As soon as the perp found out that you were an undercover cop, and we had everything on tape, he couldn't sing fast enough."

"I wish I could tell myself you'd put him away for good, but we both know the system. It's not too likely."

"It won't be for good, but it'll be a lot longer than it would have been a few years back. The courts are getting tougher and tougher on child predators. We wouldn't even be able to hold him if you hadn't set it up the way you did."

"Good. If you're done with me, I'll head on back to Gillian's."

"Yes, good idea. I'll let you know if we come up with anything that leads in the direction of Taylor."

* * *

Kelly pulled into the yard, got out of the truck and headed for the back porch. There he found Gillian, a bottle of Jack Daniels, two glasses and a bucket of ice.

Kelly sat down on the wicker love seat and put his arm around his girl. "Do you mind if I don't talk about it?."

Gillian picked up the bottle. "Rocks?"

Kelly nodded and she dropped in two ice cubes, poured two fingers into the glass and handed it over.

Kelly downed the whiskey in one swallow.

"I needed that."

Gillian refilled his glass and he leaned back and took a deep breath.

She placed her hands on either side of his face and took his mouth in a deep kiss. "Let's go upstairs. You can take a long hot shower and then we'll go to bed and sleep."

"Thanks. I've never felt so dirty in my life."

* * *

Later snuggled in the bed, spooned to Gillian's back, Kelly whispered into her ear. "I love you."

"You're welcome." She tightened the snuggle and before long sleep overtook them both.

Chapter Ten

The *Battle Hymn of the Republic* had Kelly diving for his pants and yanking out his cell phone.

"What the hell," he growled, flipping open the case and shaking the sleep out of his head.

"If you want to know about that asshole who took those pictures, you need to get on out here." Ajax shouted over the sound of a revving Harley.

"The Clubhouse?"

"Yeah. Get a move on. Scott Danforth knows the scumbag, but he's leaving for Sturgis this afternoon, so you got questions you better get 'em asked."

"I'll be there in half an hour." Kelly tossed the phone back on his pants and headed for the shower.

Ten minutes later, dressed and downstairs, he stopped in Gillian's office, scrawled "Gone to Hurst" on the yellow pad she kept on her desk, and headed outside.

Jake, who'd been keeping himself busy in the stables, tore up the porch and barked a welcome. Kelly stopped long enough to give the dog a few scratches and hug his neck.

They strolled down the steps and along the path to the truck. "Guess I'll see you tonight," Kelly said, when Jake stopped at the gate. Jake gave a short bark and turned towards the stables.

I'm going to have to investigate what's keeping him so interested out there. Kelly decided as he climbed into Old Blue and started along the driveway.

* * *

Half an hour later Kelly pulled up in front of the clubhouse and cut his engine. The garage doors stood open and several bikers stood around an antique chopper.

Ajax separated himself from the group and approached Kelly.

"That's Scott." He said, pointing at a gangly red haired biker who had started towards them when Ajax waved his arm.

"Scott." Ajax shouted over the revving Harley. "Tell Jake about that Sam character who came to the barbecue last weekend."

"Not a lot to tell." Scott stuck his hands in his pockets. "Doug Gillespie brought him along." Scott spit out a stream of chewing tobacco and wiped his mouth on his sleeve. "Guy was a Yankee. Didn't like him myself. Too slippery."

"Yeah, we know. You don't like Yankees." Ajax chimed in. "Tell Jake about the cards. Hell, show him yours."

Scott scowled and reached into his pocket for his wallet. "Like I told Ajax, Doug and this creep were pushing to get votes for a drug deal. Everyone knew that. Like we'd vote on something that stupid without Ajax here. Not if we wanted our skin we wouldn't."

Ajax nodded approval and motioned for Scott to hand over the card.

"He told us we could get 'em as young as we liked and they'd do whatever we liked too."

Kelly took the card. It was black with white calligraphy style print. The pictured showed an Elephant sitting on the back of a Turtle with the words *White Elephant Club* printed beneath. "You haven't used yours."

Scott spat tobacco again. "I got kids. Stupid Yankee bastard. Meant to throw it out but forgot about it 'til Ajax started asking questions."

Kelly nodded. "Mind if I keep this?"

"Hell no. Like I said, I'd a thrown it out if I'd remembered."

They talked a few minutes longer. Kelly attempted to get the names of some of the others who'd received cards, but Scott went mute and Kelly let it go, knowing that Gus would get the information out of him quick enough if it was needed.

"Sure didn't figure that Sam character for the brains of the operation," Scott remarked. "I kind of figured the old guy was in charge."

"What old guy?"

"Some skinny dude with white hair and chin whiskers. They called him Doc."

"Would you recognize him if you saw him again."

"I guess so." Scott didn't look too happy at the idea of identifying someone for the cops, but a look from Ajax kept him cooperative.

"I'm pretty sure I know who 'Doc' is," Kelly said when he and Ajax stepped outside. "Can you make sure Scott will be available if Gus needs him to make an identification?"

"He'll be back next weekend. He's just making a rally run. What about Sam, you want us to keep looking?"

"Yes, but if you find him call me or Gus. Don't try anything on your own."

Ajax nodded, and Kelly hoped he'd follow instructions, but it would definitely depend on what they caught Sam doing when they tracked him down. Still it was worth the risk. The bikers could ask questions in places where neither he nor Gus would get any answers.

"Keep in touch." Kelly headed for his truck and Ajax went back into the Clubhouse.

* * *

Back in his truck, Kelly called Gus and briefed him on the meeting with Scott, keeping the best for last. "You'll never guess who was out at one of their barbecues last weekend?"

"Okay, I won't guess. Who was it?"

"None other than our too smart for his own good veterinarian."

"You don't say. I guess it's time we paid the doctor an official visit. I don't even know if we ran his prints. We'll rectify that."

"Good idea. It's beginning to look like there's a more to the doctor's involvement then we've been led to believe."

"The shit we found at that Club, together with the eye witness' testimony to the doctor's involvement we should be able to get a warrant for the vet's house and clinic. I'll get someone started on that right away. Meantime why don't you grab Gillian and come on out to the house? Betty's planning to barbecue up some rib eyes tonight and she's been nagging the devil out of me to have you bring that girl of yours out for a visit."

"As if I could resist Betty's cooking. It'll be good for Gillian to take a break too. I'm going to stop by Indian Creek on my way back to town, Cam and Stella got back from Oregon last night and I want to touch base with them. I'll give Gillian a call and let her know about tonight. What time do you want us there?"

"Let's say four-thirty. I'll set the wheels in motion regarding the doctor and depending on what comes back, we'll either pick him up or let him stew. Either way I'll be heading home out by three."

"Sounds good."

"Give my regards to Cam and Stella."

"Will do. Catch you later." Kelly stuck his phone back in his pocket and headed Old Blue towards Indian Creek.

* * *

Later, back at the ranch, Kelly went in search of Gillian and found her out in the stables helping Robin.

"Hi there." She called when she spotted him standing in the open doorway. "Give me a minute to get this mare settled and I'll be right with you."

"Take your time." Kelly grinned. "There's something very soothing about watching a couple of attractive ladies pitch hay."

"A smart man is very careful of his comments when faced with a couple of women holding pitchforks." Gillian winked at Robin and both of them laughed.

"I get the point…bad pun intended." Kelly laughingly turned on his heel and headed toward the house. "Gus has invited us for dinner," he called over his shoulder.

After stopping for a chat and a dog rub with Jake, Kelly let himself into the house and headed upstairs for a shower and a change of clothes.

Later, Kelly snagged a long neck from the fridge and joined the dog on the back porch.

"You sure have settled yourself in around here," Kelly remarked, taking a seat on the swing and letting his hand trail along the dog's back.

The two of them relaxed and dozed in the comfortable silence that comes from long companionship. The better part of an hour had passed when Gillian let herself into the kitchen, grabbed a cold one from the refrigerator, and settled into the swing beside Kelly.

"Seems like I've caught myself a cat nap," Kelly said, slipping his arm around her shoulder.

"I passed Jake heading back to the barn."

"There wouldn't happen to be a female lurking anywhere around those parts would there?"

Gillian laughed. "As a matter of fact the Robertson's female has been spending a lot more time around here since Jake's been in residence."

"Figures. So how's it going out there? Is Robin doing okay with the change of schedule?"

"She's doing great. It was nice today. We got a lot done. Of course we all still have the murders in the back of our minds, but this is probably the first day we didn't talk about them. We concentrated on the horses, and our plans for the fall – normal stuff."

"I'm glad. I know how badly you want things back to normal and I'm hoping it's not going to be too much longer. Although I do have to tell you something that isn't going to make you very happy."

Gillian closed her eyes for a moment and then lifted her head. "I guess I'd better hear it now."

"I'm afraid one of your people may not be quite what they seem. I hate bringing it up, but you need to be forewarned."

"Is it Dr. Morgan?"

"Now how did you come up with that?"

Gillian shook her head. "I don't know. Maybe it's instinct, or more likely it's a combination of that and some of the things he's said that don't quite jive."

"You better be careful or we'll have you turned into a detective."

"No thanks. Once this stuff is finished I intend to stay a long ways away from anything to do with the business side of your life."

Kelly laughed and pulled her into his arms. After a satisfactory diversion from the subject at hand, he leaned her head against his shoulder. "I hope it won't be much longer. I've got a feeling we're getting close. Gus is running background on Dr. Morgan this afternoon, so if anything pops we'll know about it tonight."

"Thank heavens he finished up with our horses this morning. I don't think I could face him now that I know you he might have been involved in what happened to those boys."

"I doubt he'll come back here, however, if it'll

make you feel better I'll ask Gus to have someone keep an eye on the place."

"Would you?"

"You bet. I'll give Gus a call while you go get changed for dinner. How's that?"

She leaned in and gave him a kiss. "Thanks." She rose from the swing and prepared to head upstairs.

"Better be careful with those hot kisses or I'll be joining you up there."

Gillian laughed. "Later. First we have a barbecue. I'm looking forward to meeting Gus' wife."

"Betty's a dream. I've been telling him for years he's just lucky he saw her first. She's also one of the best cooks in Texas, so we'll need to bring our appetites."

"My stomach heard that one. I'll be quick."

* * *

Kelly took out his cell and pressed speed dial for Gus.

"I was just on my way out the door." The detective sounded rushed. "I've news, but it can wait until I see you at the house."

"That's what I was calling about. Any chance you can get someone to keep an eye on the ranch while Gillian and I are away? She's real uncomfortable knowing her vet might be involved in all this."

"He's involved all right. That's what we'll be talking about tonight. I'll send someone right over. Darn good idea. Especially since we don't know where the good doctor is right now."

"Sounds like things are popping."

Gus grunted.

Kelly chuckled. "Okay. It'll wait until after dinner. Tell Betty I'm bringing my appetite."

* * *

Gus and Betty lived in what used to be a rural area on the Arlington side of Fort Worth. The urban sprawl of the past decade had brought the city out to the country. Rush hour traffic was already in full swing by the time Kelly and Gillian headed out, but Kelly pulled off I-30 and followed a winding maze of streets that only a local would recognize. In no time at all they were out of the city and approaching Arlington. At Morningside Drive Kelly followed a tree-lined road to the end where he turned in and parked behind Gus' unmarked but unmistakable Crown Vic.

The neat little rambler where Gus and Betty had raised three kids and an assortment of dogs, cats and rabbits looked pretty much the same as it had the last time Kelly had pulled into the familiar driveway.

"What a friendly looking house," Gillian said.

Kelly nodded. "I couldn't describe it better myself." He sat for a moment, both hands on the wheel, while pictures of the past flooded his mind, then, forcing himself to let go of the wheel, he turned to Gillian and brought his mind back to the present.

Gillian smiled and squeezed his arm and Kelly returned her smile.

Gus and Betty had been two of Lynda's favorite

people. A lot of years had passed since then, and Kelly had gradually moved on with his life, but being here, at Gus and Betty's had jogged some bittersweet memories and he appreciated the fact that Gillian seemed to understand.

"Shall we go see what's for dinner?" Kelly reached across and opened Gillian's door.

"I'm starved." She climbed out of the truck.

Betty was already on the front porch waving a dish towel, and Kelly had no sooner started up the steps than she had her chubby arms around his neck and was planting a kiss on his cheek.

"It's about time you decided to bring this young lady out here to your adopted mama."

Kelly reached back and grasped Gillian hand. "I'd like you to meet Gillian. She's the special lady in my life."

Betty opened her arms and pulled Gillian into the hug. "I'm so very glad to meet you." She smiled into Gillian's eyes and the two shared an instant connection.

"Would you like to join me in the kitchen, while I send this one back to Gus' study?" Betty asked and when Gillian responded with an eager, "yes please," Betty turned to Kelly and motioned down the hall. "You know where he is," she said, taking Gillian's arm and heading for the kitchen.

* * *

Kelly went straight to the study where he found Gus stretched out in the same well-worn leather recliner that he'd had for as long as Kelly could remember.

"There's a cold one in the holder." Gus pointed to Betty's chair.

Kelly crossed the room, sank down into the soft cushioned chair, raised his legs onto the flower print footstool Betty kept parked in front of her chair, and took a long swig out of the cold bottle Gus had waiting.

Gus took a swig from his own bottle, and waited until Kelly set his down before getting down to business.

"Once I told the judge we had an eye witness who was prepared to swear the doctor was involved in that child pornography and maybe even human trafficking operation, being run out of the *White Elephant*, he couldn't give us a warrant fast enough."

"But?" Kelly knew there had to be a '*but*' because Gus' tone was anything but satisfied.

"Son of a bitch must have been tipped off, either that or he figured we'd get around to doing some digging sooner or later. I'm kicking my own ass for not doing it sooner."

"I guess that means he was already in the system?"

"Yes and no." Gus shook his head. "It wasn't as if he'd have popped up in the normal course. The boys had checked his credentials as a matter of course, when his name first came up, but everything appeared to be in order. What they didn't do, however, because there wasn't any reason to at the time, was have the Veterinary Licensing Board send over a picture. That's what I did this afternoon, and imagine my surprise when Dr. Morgan, DVM, could have been one of my own relatives."

"You're kidding?"

"Nope. Definitely a black man, and about fifteen years younger than the Dr. Morgan we've been dealing with."

Kelly scowled. "I don't get it. He's been looking after Gillian's horses for a couple of years now. She may not be medically trained, but she's a smart woman and there's no way she'd have been fooled by someone who didn't have any medical knowledge."

"Oh the good doctor had plenty of medical knowledge." Gus slapped his hand on the arm of his chair. "Once we knew the doctor was a fake, I sent his prints over to the Feds. Of course we all know hindsight is 20/20, but I sure as hell wish I'd done that first thing."

Kelly had slid forward in his chair, his eyes fixed on Gus' face.

"They tagged him."

"Sure as hell did. Here take a look at this." Gus handed over a sheet of paper with a picture that Kelly instantly recognized as Dr. Morgan.

State of North Carolina
WANTED

Dr. Frank Bollinger. Wanted for questioning in the sexual molestation and murder of five year old Carter Salinger.

"I should have listened to my gut." Kelly handed the paper back to Gus. "There was something about his story that just didn't fit. Damn it to hell. I guess you've called North Carolina?"

"Damn right. Matter of fact, a couple of their detectives will be here in the morning. It's been fifteen years, but the case is still an open sore for them. It seems the doctor was spotted with the boy, but he claimed to have been a Good Samaritan. Said he saw the boy walking along the road and gave him a ride. The boy lived out in the country, and the doctor supposedly dropped him off at the corner leading to his house. It was one of those country places set back about a quarter mile from the road. His story sounded plausible and nobody thought much about it. The doctor was well respected in the community and it wouldn't have been out of character for him to give the boy a ride."

"So what happened to change their minds?"

"A couple of hunters downed a doe in the exact spot where the boy's body had been buried. After they gutted the deer, they dug a hole to bury the entrails and hit one of the boy's leg bones with the shovel."

"Guess it's a good thing they knew the difference between human and animal."

"Oh yeah. These two were ex-Marines. They called the sheriff and all hell broke loose. The body had been there several months, but the medical examiner confirmed that the boy had been sexually abused. For a smart man the doctor made a pretty stupid mistake. He wrapped the boy in one of the blankets he kept in his own car. He must have realized his mistake later but he didn't dare risk going back to the body."

"I suppose he cleared out as soon as he heard the body'd been found?"

"That's just what he did. His taking off like that

made him look guilty as hell, but he probably realized there was enough evidence on the body to hang him. I bet when they finish digging into this they'll find that the real Dr. Morgan was actually a patient of this Bollinger's. He might have died of natural causes, or maybe he was helped along. We may never know."

"So Dr. Bollinger simply walked out of his old life and into the life of Dr. Morgan, veterinarian."

"That's about it. Apparently he took off some time last night."

"Are they sure he's gone?"

"Oh they're sure. All his papers and personal effects are gone."

Kelly shook his head. "I never thought to tell Scott to keep his story to himself – not that it would have done any good anyhow."

"At that point we were looking for information from all of them, you wouldn't have had any reason to try and keep Scott's story under wraps. Likely he'd already told them anyhow. What about Ajax? You figure he might know who spilled the beans to the doctor?"

"That's exactly what I was planning to find out." Kelly nodded his head towards the doorway. "I don't want to spoil Betty's dinner, and it probably isn't going to make a lot of difference if I get hold of him now or later, but with your approval, I'll run Gillian home after we're done here and then pay another visit out to that Clubhouse."

"You don't think a phone call will do the trick?"

"I don't want to chance it. Ajax told me they were having a general meeting tonight and he intended to find out if anyone else knew anything about Sam and his whereabouts. At this point I have no reason not to trust Ajax, but I'll feel a hell of a lot better if I'm looking him in the eye when I ask my questions."

"Good timing." Gus said, when Betty poked her head around the corner and beckoned for them to come to the table.

The hour that followed consisted of friendly table conversation, and lots of lip smacking while they consumed double thick rib eye steaks, and corn on the cob dripping with butter.

They had finished the main course and everyone was digging into heaping portions of strawberry shortcake when Kelly's phone started buzzing against his pant leg.

"I'm sorry. Do you mind excusing me for just a minute?" He offered a rueful apology to Betty, who only smiled and motioned for him to go take his call. A typical cop's wife, she was used to interrupted dinners.

"Hang on," Kelly said into the receiver, after seeing Ajax's number flash on the screen, "I'll take this outside," he said with a nod to Gus, who pushed back his chair and followed him outside."

"What's up?" Kelly put the phone back to his ear.

"We've got that bastard surrounded and if you want him in one piece you better get the cavalry and get the hell out here."

"Who you got, Sam or the doctor?"

"Doctor. What in hell do we want with the doctor? I thought you wanted that Yankee pervert whose been messing with our kids?"

"Yes, we do. Where are you?"

"Out at the Webster place at the end of Lone Star Road. You know where it is?"

"Hang on." Kelly held the phone out to Gus. "They've got Sam trapped in a house out at the end of Lone Star Road."

"Ajax," Gus roared into the phone. "This is Detective Graham. There'll be a unit out there within ten minutes and I'll be right behind them. You just make sure he stays inside the house until we get there. And, mind you keep your boys from killing him. We need that asshole alive."

Gus tossed the phone back to Kelly and headed for his car. "Tell Betty I'll be back later," he said over his shoulder. "You might as well take Gillian on home. I'll call you as soon as we know something."

Chapter Eleven

"I still can't believe it." Gillian said as they drove towards the ranch. "I've seen and talked to that monster almost every day for years, and never once suspected what he was. What's the matter with me, don't I have any instincts?"

"Don't be so hard on yourself. He's a psychopath, and they fool the experts all the time. Why do you think serial killers get away with their crimes for years. Remember Ted Bundy? Everyone who knew him swore he was the 'nicest man they'd ever met'."

"I know. What you're saying makes perfectly logical sense. I just can't help feeling like I should have known, or at least suspected."

"Hey didn't you guess who I was talking about as soon as I told you someone wasn't what they seemed?"

Gillian laughed. "Okay. I did start to get a bit uneasy, but I sure wish I'd felt that way before Larry and Toby. Do you think he killed them?"

"I don't know. Depends on why. If he's what we think he is, then he wouldn't hesitate if they posed a threat, but we still don't know about this Sam character."

"So you believe Dr. Morgan – or whatever his name really is, is a psychopath."

"Yes I do. I'm not a psychiatrist, but I've dealt with enough psychos during my time on the force, and he's got all characteristics."

"It's all so ugly."

"I know, and it's probably going to get uglier

before it gets better, but at least now we know who we're looking for, and don't ever forget, Gus is very good at his job."

Gillian leaned over and placed her head against his shoulder. "And so are you Kelly McWinter. I'm just glad I've got both of you in my camp."

Kelly smiled and lifted his hand to rub her hair. "I'd say we've got each other, and from the looks of things all's quiet at the ranch."

Gillian lifted her head from his shoulder and looked out the window. They'd just pulled into the driveway, and true to Gus' word, a police car pulled in behind them.

Kelly rolled down the window and leaned out. "Thanks Paul," he said to the officer behind the wheel. "I'm going to drop Gillian off and then head out for awhile. I'd appreciate it if you'd stick around."

"My orders are to stay here until I get called off, so you go right ahead." The officer lifted his hand in a wave and Kelly turned back to Gillian.

"You don't mind if I take off for awhile do you?"

"Of course not. I'm just fine. Actually more than anything I'm madder than hell." She smiled and tossed her head as if to shake off her own emotions.

"Good. You stay that way, it'll keep you cautious. I've a hunch where the doctor might be found, and since Gus is taking care of Sam and can handle that just fine without my help, I'm going to listen to my gut and take a run out to Indian Creek. I've got my cell, if anything at all bothers you."

Gillian gave him a solemn look. "Like if I want you to pick up some groceries?"

Kelly laughed. "Glad to see you haven't lost your sense of humor. Okay funny girl, inside with you. I'm not moving until I see that door close, and lock it behind you, okay."

"Yes sir." She leaned over, kissed him on the lips and hopped out of the truck.

Jake, who had heard the truck, loped up to the driver's door and waited for Kelly.

"Hey boy. You stay here and watch her." Kelly leaned out the window and spoke to the dog.

Without a second glance Jake caught up with Gillian and followed her up the steps of the porch.

"Keep him inside," Kelly called, "he'll let you know if anything's amiss."

Gillian turned around, smiled and waved at Kelly and then opened the door for Jake to precede her into the kitchen.

* * *

This is playing one hell of a hunch, Kelly told himself, as he headed towards Indian Creek. It might be a complete waste of time, but, it wouldn't hurt to have backup, just in case, and Cam had been laying around honeymooning for weeks, so Kelly didn't have any qualms about rousting his buddy out of his honeymoon haze. Of course, he'd have to contend with Stella, but after a month of non-stop togetherness, even the volatile redhead ought to be reasonably malleable.

* * *

Cam's place, The Hideaway Bar & Barbecue, was one of the fixtures at Indian Creek. It had been in operation – in one form or another – since before Texas joined the Union— and there were those who still considered that to be the result of a plot that no true Texan woulda been party to if they hadn't been bamboozled by some damn Yankees.

There were half a dozen vehicles parked out front – a couple of pickups, a motorcycle and three cars. *Regulars,* Kelly observed as he let himself out of the truck and climbed the steps.

"Hey, look who's here." A loud chortle greeted Kelly when he stepped through the door.

"How's it going Doug?' Kelly acknowledged the old timer, and walked over to the bar.

"So how's the blushing bridegroom," he said, reaching across the counter and slapping Cam on the arm.

"What the – that's supposed to be blushing bride." Cam gave his best imitation of a growl, then he laughingly dropped the towel he'd been holding and grabbed Kelly's hand.

"Wondered when you were gonna get out here and welcome me home."

"I'm about to do more than that," Kelly lowered his voice. "I've come to spring you."

"You've what?" Cam raised his eyebrows in the quizzical look he liked to adopt whenever anybody said something he regarded as weird.

"You heard me. Where's that red head?" Kelly looked around to make sure the coast was clear, and then leaned across the counter.

"Get that pistol you finally got a license for and bring it along. Better tell Stella you're going to help me on a case, or she might come tearing along after you and ruin everything."

Cam's face split into a huge grin, and Kelly knew he had a sale. There was nothing his cowboy friend liked better than being included in one of Kelly's investigations.

"You after another killer?"

"A psychopath. I'm hoping to catch one in a trap so you know this is dangerous business."

"You think you know where to find this guy?"

"It's just a hunch, but my gut keeps telling me I'm on the right track."

"No way I'd ever bet against your gut. Can you hang on while I run back to the house and get Stella to watch the place? I'll warn her that you're on a case and you've got to get out of here in a hurry so she doesn't bombard you with questions as soon as she walks in the door."

"Just to keep you honest, I'll wait in the truck. That way you won't be lying when you tell her I don't have time to talk right now."

Cam grinned. "Be right back."

"Oh wait. Grab a couple of fishing poles and your tackle box?"

Cam turned and gave Kelly a funny look. "Now how in the hell am I supposed to explain that to Stella?"

Kelly just grinned and shaking his head Cam headed out the back door of the bar and across the lot to the small house that he and Stella now called home.

* * *

Before turning off I-30 onto Lone Star Road, Gus pulled over, grabbed his blue light out of the trunk plopped it on the roof and hit his siren. Two official cars had already arrived on the scene and apparently Ajax had kept his word and held the bikers back. It took Gus another five minutes to reach the end of the road, and there wasn't any doubt which house was the target.

Harley Davidsons of every size and description covered the yard, and a couple of patrol cars blocked the driveway.

Gus pulled in and parked behind them.

"What's the situation?" He asked a young deputy who stood beside a rusted old gate.

"We haven't seen or heard anything since we've been here, Sir."

"Okay. I'm going to talk to Ajax, and depending on what he has to say, I'll approach the front door. You watch for my signal. If you see me lift my arm like I'm about to toss a baseball, you grab your partner and take up positions on either side of that front porch."

"Yes sir." The deputy turned and headed over to the gate where his partner stood watching the bikers.

Gus shoved the gate back on its one good hinge and walked down an overgrown path of dirt and weeds to the foot of the steps where Ajax had apparently driven his bike and parked.

"What's happening?" Gus asked.

"Nothing as far as I can tell. Piss ant's probably hiding underneath the bed."

"You sure he's in there?"

"Hell yes I'm sure. Doug over there talked him into coming out on the front porch when we first got here." Ajax waved his hand at a young biker, who looked to be in his early twenties.

Gus turned to the biker, who had his eyes trained on the ground like he'd suddenly lost something.

"You the one that's been bringing Sam around?"

The biker shrugged and Gus walked over to get in his face. "You don't hear so good?"

"I heard. A friend of mine hooked me up with the guy a couple months ago. Seemed okay. I been showing him around a bit."

"I just bet you have. We'll talk about that later. Right now I want you to go on up there to the front door. Tell your buddy that a detective with the Tarrant County Sherriff's Department is out front and wants to have a little chat."

Doug lifted both hands in an empty gesture and shrugged again. "He ain't gonna listen to me now he's spooked."

"You just do what I tell you. Get on up there to the door and you tell him that he's got two choices. Either he walks out here on his own two feet and I take him into custody, nice and safe, or I drive the hell on out of here and let Ajax and his boys take him into custody the hard way. Up to him."

"You can't do that."

"Who the fuck you telling what they can't do." Gus stuck his face up eye to eye with the now badly shaken biker and leaned forward. "You going?"

Doug did a jump and turn, and headed for the porch at a fast lope.

"Probably pissed his pants." Ajax said from behind Gus. "You mean that about me'n the boys taking him down for you?"

Gus held his hand up for silence and watched as Doug approached the front door, stopped and knocked hard.

"Hey Sam." Doug yelled loud enough to be heard out on the road. "It's me Doug. Look you gotta come out here now."

A muffled voice could be heard coming from inside the house, and after a few seconds of listening Doug spoke again.

"I'm not shitting you man. You need to come out here now. There's a murder cop out here who says he's going give you about 10 more minutes to get your ass outside, or he's going to head on back to town and tell Ajax and the boys to bring you in by any means they want to use."

More indecipherable sounds from inside the house, while Doug pressed his ear against the door.

"No. I'm not messing with you man. These cops don't give a shit what happens to foreigners, especially Yankees. If you don't get your ass out here and get that detective to take you in, you stand about as much chance of staying in one piece as a rooster tossed into a cat house."

The muffled voice from the other side continued for several minutes, until Doug held up his hand and yelled to Gus.

"He wants to talk to you."

Gus lifted his arm and motioned for the two deputies to take their positions on either side of the porch.

"Tell him. I'm on my way." Gus yelled back and then turned to speak to Ajax. "You make sure your boys stay under control. Once this bird turns himself into my custody, that'll be the signal for you to crank up the bikes and ride on out of here."

Ajax nodded. "Gotcha. He's your pigeon."

* * *

Back at the Hideaway Cam climbed into the cab of Old Blue and grinned. "Feels like old times," he said, as Kelly pulled out of the driveway and headed back towards town.

"You'll probably be grinning out of the other side of your face if we do happen to track down that psychopath we're after."

"Nah. You wouldn't be looking so smug if you didn't have some kind of plan in mind."

"Smart Ass."

"So what's the plan?"

"Remember that old fishing shack Bubba took us to out there where the Trinity dumps into Eagle Mountain Lake?"

"Sure, but I haven't been out there in a couple of years. Don't even know if it's still standing."

"Yeah. That's one of the things we're gambling on. The other is that I'm right about the doctor's hideout." Kelly let up on the gas and prepared to make a left turn off of Boat Club Road onto Peden.

"You thinking the doctor might he holed up at Larry's mother's old place?"

"I think it's a possibility."

"But I heard the old lady gave that place over to some clinic where she left her cat."

"Exactly. What kind of clinic do you think a veterinarian is likely to have?"

"Damn." Cam slapped his hand to his forehead. "It never even occurred to me to put clinic and vet together and come up with your missing psychopath. Guess that's why you're the Sherlock and I'm just a Watson."

Kelly indulged in a good belly laugh, and then turned the conversation back to the project ahead of them.

"First off I've got to get Old Blue hidden. The doctor knows me, and he knows my truck. So that's no good."

"I guess that's where I get to prove my usefulness."

"Only if you're damn sure you want a part of this." Kelly's voice turned serious. "I can't think of any reason why you should be in any danger if you do exactly what we discuss…"

"I'll be fine," Cam interrupted, but Kelly put up his hand.

"Wait, let me finish. This doctor's a psychopath. He's already killed a small boy and probably two of Gillian's workers. We're not going to take any chances on you becoming another victim."

"You worry too much."

Kelly shook his head and scowled. "And just who in the hell do you think is going to have to deal with that redhead if anything happened to you? I'd rather tangle with a dozen psychopaths than have that hotheaded bride of yours after my tail."

Cam shook with laughter. "Guess you got a point there. Okay, what's the plan?"

"From what I can remember that fishing shack is about a quarter mile from the old Preston place."

"Sounds about right." Cam agreed. There's an old logging road comes off of Peden about a mile before you get to the cabin. It's full of ruts and probably overgrown with branches, but if you don't mind risking Old Blue's fenders, we ought to be able to follow that far enough in to get the truck hidden. If that's what you had in mind."

"Perfect. We'll hide the truck and then hike on in the rest of the way. Never mind the dings, I won't mind a few nicks if it'll help us get that maniac out of circulation."

* * *

A subdued Sam Taylor sat inside a small room with a table, two chairs and a one way mirror through which Gus and Miles Stanton, the homicide division supervisor, stood watching him sweat.

"You figure him for the killings?" Stanton, a tall man with dark thinning hair was dressed in a medium brown suit. His role of cop supervisor and chief paper pusher fit him well.

Gus shook his head. "Maybe the Preston killing. That one was probably unplanned. Preston either saw or overheard something he shouldn't have and confronted Taylor. Maybe he threatened to tell Gillian. That would support Angelina's story. She claims Preston intended to come clean when Gillian got back from holidays. I guess we'll never know exactly what happened, but I'm going to try and get Taylor to admit he hit Preston over the head. The CSI's found blood and hair on one of the shovels in the stables and we're going on the assumption that's the murder weapon."

"Sounds like you're on the right track. What about the other boy?"

"I'm betting on the doctor for that one. I'd say Toby was lured somewhere by the doctor, probably on the pretense that the he had information about Preston's death – everyone thinks they're better equipped to solve a crime than the police. Once the doctor got Toby to the location, he hit him over the head – probably hoping Larry's killer would be blamed – and dumped him in the lake."

"Sounds like the murder scene is somewhere around Eagle Mountain Lake."

"Most likely. Of course that covers a lot of territory. I'm hoping Taylor can give us a lead on the doctor's whereabouts. He will if he wants to keep from swinging for the crime himself."

"I imagine if you explain to him the difference between doing time for second degree murder and ending up on death row for premeditated murder, he'll be jumping all over himself to help you pin the tail on the doctor."

"No time like the present to find out." Gus said, and leaving Miles to watch through the one way glass, he proceeded into the interrogation room.

"So Sam," Gus said, pulling out a chair. "You seem to have gotten yourself into quite a pickle."

Sam's face flushed red to the roots of his bleached blond hair. "I don't know what you're talking about. You know damn well that gang of bikers was going to skin me alive if I didn't come with you. You ain't got nothing to keep me here."

"You'll want to drop that bullshit right fast. It's all the same to me if I give you a break, or walk out of here and let the DA take over."

"What for? Nobody's accused me of anything. I got rights."

"You sure do Sam. Didn't the officers read you your rights before they brought you in here, and didn't you agree that you understood those rights?'

"Sure, but I already told you. I only did that to get away from them bikers."

"Well the bikers will be the least of your worries. Right now we have you on several counts of distributing child pornography. Plus we're investigating your connection to human trafficking, and oh yes, I can't forget murder. We have you down for two counts of murder, one of them premeditated. Guess the last one makes the others irrelevant since premeditated murder carriers the death penalty."

"Here now. I ain't murdered nobody. You guys got the wrong man here."

Gus slammed his fist down on the table and put his face right up into Taylors.

"You listen to me you piece of shit slime bag. I don't have time to mess around with you. You're locked up tight on the child porn, so don't even go there. We've opened the locker with your filthy bag of shit. Your prints are all over the contents and your pals at the *White Elephant* were only too happy to point to you as the mastermind behind this whole scheme. And, we've got your prints all over the handle of the shovel that killed Larry, so we've got you dead to rights on the first murder as well. The only thing we're questioning now is the second murder. Did you lure Toby out to the murder scene? Cause if you did then it's premeditated murder and the only question left is whether they're going to fry you in the chair or stick you in the arm."

"That's crazy. I ain't no mastermind of anything, and I didn't kill Toby. That was the doctor. When I told him what happened with Larry and that Toby had gotten in touch with me, he said for me to forget about Toby and leave everything to him. I don't know what happened after that, but I didn't have nothing to do with Toby's death."

"So you admit to killing Larry?"

"Yes. No, wait, I admit to hitting him over the head with a shovel, but I wasn't trying to kill him. I was trying to protect myself. That wasn't no murder, that was self-defense. That asshole spied on me and got the combination to the locker. He didn't have no business getting into that locker, but I know damn well he thought I had drugs in there. Stupid son-of-a-bitch was trying to rob me. Then when he found that envelope with those pictures inside, he went ballistic. Came at me like a mad man. There wasn't anything I could do. He jumped me from behind, and started to beat the shit out of me. I grabbed the shovel and whacked him over the head and got the hell out of there. I didn't know he was dead. I only whacked him with the shovel to save my own skin."

"So you hit him over the head and then left him there?"

"Yeah. Look maybe it wasn't very noble, but I didn't know he was dead, and I didn't want to stick around there and let him wake up and go after me again. He was a crazy man. Probably he'd have killed me if I hadn't gotten the hell out of there."

"So you're claiming the doctor killed Toby?"

"I guess. Like I said, I told him what happened and that Toby wanted a meeting, and he said for me to forget about it and he'd take care of Toby. That's all I know."

"I don't know. Maybe we can do something for you, and maybe not. It'll depend on what the DA thinks of your story. About the only thing that might help swing him to your side is if I can tell him you helped us find the doctor."

"I don't know where he is. What about his house? His clinic? You've got a better idea of where he might be than I have."

"If that's the best you can do, it's not likely the DA's going to be too impressed."

"What about the murder charge? I've cooperated. I'm telling the truth. You need to tell them that."

"You haven't given us anything to help us locate the doctor, so unless we get lucky, he's likely on his way out of the state and the DA's going to need to charge someone. You figure it out." Gus started for the door, and Sam yelled for him to stop before he crossed the room.

"I heard they found Toby's body out at Eagle Mountain Lake. Is that right?"

"Why, do you know something about that?"

"I know the doctor's got a place out there."

Gus walked back to the table and stood looking down at Sam. "Where?"

"I don't know where it is exactly, but it's somewhere around where Indian Creek runs into Eagle Mountain Lake. I heard Larry talking about how his old lady had a house out there but she turned it over to the doctor's clinic in exchange for lifetime care for her damn cat."

Gus turned and walked back to the door. "You sit tight. They'll be along to process you in awhile."

"That was slick." The supervisor said when Gus joined him at the window.

"Yeah. I'd say he's telling the truth. Nasty piece of slime, but he hasn't got the brains or the guts to mastermind anything. Probably happened just the way he says. We'll book him on the child porn and leave him sweat for a few days. If I had my way I'd leak the details and throw him in with the general population." Gus shook his head and held up his hand. "I know, don't screw around or we'll end up giving him a free pass."

"What about the doctor?"

"We've got an APB out on him already. There's a couple of detectives coming in from North Carolina this afternoon. If I'm not around would you mind giving them a run down and showing them everything we have on the doctor – which isn't a hell of a lot, but hopefully by the time we're done we'll have plenty more."

"Be glad to. You going to check into this lake property?"

"Kelly McWinter's from out that way. He'll know where the Preston's property is located. I'll get hold of him and we'll take a run out there. Maybe we'll get lucky and catch the doctor with his pants down."

"Keep me in the loop."

Before heading out Gus stopped by his desk in homicide to check messages and see if he could get Kelly on his cell.

* * *

Kelly and Cam had driven Old Blue as far as they dared along the road that led to the fishing camp, before tucking it away inside a grove of trees so thick you'd have to be looking in order to spot a truck.

They carried on for another five hundred feet on foot and came out at a dilapidated shack. The windows had been boarded up long ago, but a board was missing in the front door and from the scat on the floor, it was clear the interior had been used by an assortment of raccoons, rats and rabbits.

"Don't look like any humans have been inside this place since we were kids." Cam said, when Kelly pushed open the door and the two of them stepped inside.

"At least it's a not likely the doctor has been down here. That's good from our standpoint."

They stepped back outside and Kelly reached into the back of the truck and handed Cam his fishing pole and tackle box. "Let's go over this one more time just to be sure we've got our signals straight."

Cam took the fishing pole and tackle box and balanced the pole on his shoulder. "I start walking toward the house, keeping up a pretty good pace, until I get within about fifty yards, and then I slow down, look around, and act a bit uncertain, like I'm not sure of my welcome."

"Yeah. That's good. If a dog starts barking you better be prepared to hightail it into the trees."

"You think that's likely?" A worried expression crossed Cam's face and Kelly remembered that his friend had suffered a nasty mauling from a Doberman one night when he cut the dog's master off in the bar.

"It's possible, but not likely. The doctor has to be planning to get out of the state before things get too hot for him here. He's not going to want to be tied down with an animal that requires care and feeding."

"Okay, I hope you're right." Cam returned to his rehearsal. "So once I get within about ten yards of the house, I stop, put my rod and tackle box down on the ground and start hollering for the owner."

Kelly's phone buzzed against his leg and he reached in his pocket. "Good thing I remembered to turn this damn thing on vibrate," he said to Cam. "All we'd need is the *Battle Hymn of the Republic* blasting out of the woods when you're supposed to be alone out here with no phone."

Cam laughed and raised his eyes skyward.

"Hey Gus", Kelly said into the phone. "How'd you manage with Sam? You get him to spill his guts yet?"

Kelly listened and then laughed. "I wouldn't have expected any less. What did you find out about the doctor?"

More listening. "That's a damn funny coincidence. Guess where I am right now?" Kelly grinned at Cam. "Bingo. That's exactly where we are. Well, about three or four hundred yards from the house to be precise.

"No, not Gillian, I've got Cam with me. I picked him up and we came up with a plan to sneak up on the house and see if the doctor's in residence."

* * *

Kelly listened for a few minutes, then put the cell back in his pocket.

"Let's get this show on the road," he said to Cam. "Gus is on his way over with the Swat team. He's tentatively approved our plan but he wants us to hang back until he gets in position."

Cam looked at Kelly and frowned. "I thought you said get the show on the road."

"I did. Look, Gus is a terrific detective, but he's got a cop mentality. He doesn't want any civilians involved. I see his point, but I know from past experience that once the cops all get here it's very unlikely we'll be able to pull this off without somebody or something screwing it up."

"Gotcha there."

"So, I figure we go ahead as planned. Make our approach, identify the target, and then pull back. If it's the doctor, we turn our information over to Gus and get the hell out of the way. If it's some innocent resident who doesn't know squat about what's going on, we pass that information on to Gus and then get the hell out of the way. Either way, once we make our ID we're clear and the show's over as far as we're concerned."

"Sounds good. You want me to take off now?"

"Yes, but just before you get within sight of the house, stop and wait for my signal." Kelly did one of the hawk calls he'd used as kid. "When you hear that it means I'm in position and you can start your approach on the house."

Cam picked up his rod and tackle and started walking.

Kelly took his gun out of the glove box, slipped it into the pocket of his jacket and started off slightly to the right of Cam's pathway.

Fifteen minutes later Kelly approached a small stand of trees that stood at the corner of a small ranch style house.

Seen better days. Kelly noted the peeling paint and overgrown gardens, but the layout couldn't have been better for his purposes.

From behind the trees, he had a full view of the back door to the house, and if he inched around to the right, he could see most of the front yard.

Crouching, he made his hawk call and waited. A minute later he spotted Cam walking out of the woods and straight towards the house.

Good. Cam had heard the call and they were on target.

Kelly pulled back and looked towards the back door. All was secure. He inched around the corner and watched Cam place his tackle on the ground, and then he heard his friend's voice.

"Hey there. Anybody home? I could sure use some help out here. All I want is to use your telephone. Could you do a favor for a stranger?"

Silence. As Kelly watched, Cam walked closer, and repeated his request for assistance. Still no response from inside and Kelly began to wonder if they'd made a mistake. He stepped back, and looked towards the back door. No sign of life. The window closest to Kelly's hiding place looked to be uncovered. He decided to wait until Cam called out again and then make a dash for the window. Maybe he could get a glimpse inside. Sadly it looked like they might be playing to an empty stage.

"Hey there. Anybody home?" Cam's voice rang out again and Kelly dashed for the window. Flattening himself against the wall, he slowly raised himself to full height and leaned to the left. That's when he saw the doctor. Crouched beside the front window, with a pistol in his hand, there seemed little doubt of what the bastard intended. He was going to shoot Cam.

Kelly sprinted to the right, rounded the building and yelled for Cam to drop to the ground, just as the first shot rang out.

"You okay?" Kelly yelled.

"Yeah. I'm good." Cam's panting voice brought a surge of relief to Kelly.

"Can you get to cover?"

"I'm there." Cam called from behind an old wishing well that featured the remains of what must have been a flower garden at one time.

"Maybe you could give him something to think about while I try and make my way oughta here."

"You got it." Kelly slipped back to his former position at the window and aimed his pistol. The doctor had taken up a position at the front window, but Kelly could just glimpse him from the rear.

Not bothering with aiming, he fired a volley of shot straight through the window, guaranteed to distract anyone inside.

"Let's get the hell out of here." Cam's voice came from the grove of trees, and Kelly whirled and ran to join his friend in the trees.

Sirens in the distance assured the two men that their exchange of gunfire had been heard. No doubt Gus and his entourage would be arriving before the doctor got too far away.

"Time for us to make ourselves scarce." Kelly said, and Cam suited action to the request by standing up and heading straight back into the woods that had brought them there.

Kelly pulled his cell phone out of his pocket and punched the speed dial for Gus.

"What the hell's going on out here?" Gus' voice blasted Kelly's eardrum.

"The doctor's in the house. We got a look at him, but he started shooting and we got the hell out of there. You enroute?"

Kelly held the phone back from his ear, as Gus' voice roared through the receiver.

"Yeah. Sorry about that. We just wanted to identify the occupant. Didn't expect him to start shooting at a stranger with a fishing pole. Anyway, no use hollering about spilled milk. He's in there. I shot a dozen rounds through the back window. We didn't stick around to find out if I hit anything, but if he ain't in there now he hasn't gone far."

More yelling while Kelly grinned at the phone. "Good. We're heading back to the Hideaway." He said, putting the phone back to his ear. "Let me know what goes down."

Kelly pocketed his phone and followed Cam out of the woods and into the clearing beside the shack.

"Just a mite riled was he?" Cam grinned as Kelly came alongside.

"He'll get over it. Like I told you, he's not fond of civilians in the mix, but he knows that having a positive ID on the doctor gives him a hell of an advantage. The occupant fired on a couple of innocent passersby, so that gives the cops the right to go in there with whatever force needed and flush the bastard out. They won't need to negotiate, so if the doctor hasn't gotten himself the hell out of there already, they'll have him wrapped up before we get back home."

"Good. You've definitely livened my day up a bit with this little adventure of yours, but I gotta confess the Hideaway's sounding real good right about now. What say we take Gus' advice and get ourselves the hell outta here."

Kelly nodded agreement and the two of them headed down the trail to the spot where they'd hidden Old Blue.

* * *

After leaving the Hideaway Kelly stopped at Luigi's for a pizza and arrived home just as Robin was leaving."

"Early night tonight?" He asked when Gillian joined him on the back porch.

"Robin has tickets to the Sugarland concert, so I told her I'd take care of settling the brood mares. What about you, have you heard from Gus?"

"No. I waited around the Hideaway for a couple of hours, but no calls. Until they wrap and tie things up he won't be thinking about anything else. We'll just have to wait. Don't worry though. Gus has Sam locked up and he won't rest until he's got the doctor in there beside him."

"Maybe by next week things can start to get back to normal."

"I hope so. Although I've gotten real used to the sleeping arrangements around here. It'll be tough getting back to just me and Jake in that old cabin."

"Oh, the poor suffering bachelors." Gillian laughingly grabbed another slice of pizza. "I need to go settle the mares for the night. What do you say to dishing up a couple of bowls of that peach cobbler you'll find in the fridge. It won't take me a minute and I should be back just in time to catch the ice cream before it melts."

"Whoa. Yes ma'am. You definitely know all my weaknesses."

Kelly grabbed the plates and pizza box and headed for the kitchen while Gillian snagged her jacket off of the rack in the corner and headed for the stables.

After filling the bowls and bringing them out to the table, Kelly settled back in his chair to wait. Minutes passed and ice cream started to slide.

Damn, can't have that. Kelly took a spoon and cleaned up the sides of his bowl while looking longingly at Gillian's. *I'll give her another five and then both bowls are going to be at risk.* He grinned at the possibility of having to eat both bowls to save them from a meltdown.

A shot rang out from the direction of the stables. Kelly leapt out of his chair, grabbed the gun out of his jacket pocket and slapped the screen door open.

"What the damn hell?" He yelled as he raced towards the brood barn, where Jake, alerted by the gunshot, stood in front of the closed doors barking like a beast gone rabid.

"Easy boy," Kelly said, approaching the door with his weapon drawn. "Gilly, you okay in there?" Kelly reached the door and pulled the handle. It held fast. Someone had apparently locked it from inside.

"Gillian?" Kelly called in a voice laced with fear and Jake once again started his frantic barking.

"Okay. Stand down." Kelly spoke to the dog, then placed his ear against the door and listened.

From inside came the sounds of sobbing.

"Gillian." Kelly yelled again. "For God's sake, open the door."

Footsteps, and then the creaking sound of the latch being shoved back. Kelly shoved and in seconds he was through the door and holding Gillian in his arms.

"What happened?"

"I shot him." She sobbed and pointed towards a figure lying half in and half out of one of the holding pens.

"Wait here." Kelly approached the body, recognized the doctor and pressed his fingers against the fugitive's neck.

"He's not going anywhere," Kelly said, walking back to Gillian and pulling her into his arms. "Are you hurt?"

"No. I'm okay." She buried her head against his chest and burst into tears.

Finally, the sobbing decreased and she lifted her head. "He was hiding in the tack room," she said, wiping her nose on the handkerchief Kelly handed over.

"Thank God you put that gun on the shelf. I was giving Misty her grain when I heard someone in the tack room. I almost called out. I don't know what stopped me, but I guess it was knowing Gus hadn't called about the doctor. I pretended I was talking to Misty. "Wait a minute," I said. "I'll get the clippers and take care of that hoof." Then I let myself out of the stall and walked over to the shelf. I grabbed the gun, and turned around and there he was, coming towards me." Gillian sobs broke through her voice and Kelly rubbed her back.

"It's okay," he said. "Take your time."

"I pointed the gun at him and told him again to stop. He just laughed at me. "You're not going to use that," he said, and I knew if I didn't pull the trigger then he'd have me and it would be all over. You should have seen the look in his eyes. He was like a crazy man."

Kelly hugged her tight and whispered into her hair. "If you hadn't pulled that trigger it would be you lying on the floor over there, not him. You did what had to be done, and I'm real proud of you for having the guts."

Gillian smiled through her tears. "Thanks. It doesn't feel very good to know I killed a man, but I'm glad it's finally over."

Kelly laid his cheek against the top of her head. "We need to call Gus. Do you think you can sit down over there on that bale and wait while I get him on the phone?"

Gillian nodded. "I'll be okay. I know you need me to stay here until Gus comes and processes the scene. It's okay Kelly. I know he has to make sure it really was self-defense."

* * *

Hours later after the crime scene team had finished their work and Gus had given his okay for Gillian and Kelly to wait for him on back to the back porch, the couple sat huddled together on the love seat.

"I know this is a hell of a time." Kelly lifted Gillian onto his lap and titled her chin so they were looking into each other's eyes, "but I have a question to ask you."

"I hope it isn't anything that's going to make me unhappy." Her smile faded. "I don't know how many of those 'guts' you were talking about me having that I've got left."

Kelly laughed and pressed his lips against hers. "I hope it won't make you unhappy." He broke the kiss and looked back into her eyes.

"I'm not down on one knee," he said cuddling her against him, "but I think this is better. Gillian, would you do me the honor of becoming my wife?"

Gillian's eyes flew open and she grabbed his shoulders with her hands. "What did you say? Do you really mean it? Oh my God, Kelly, I never dreamed you were thinking of marriage. Kelly McWinter, you've just made me the happiest woman in Texas."

"I guess that's a yes." Kelly laughed and bent his head for a very long and enthusiastically returned kissing session.

"Ahem." Gus' voice broke in just at the point where a trip to the bedroom would definitely have been required.

Kelly lifted his head and grinned. "Maybe not the best timing in the world," he said, "but we've been through one hell of a tough couple of weeks, and I'd like you to be the first to meet my future wife." He lifted Gillian off his lap and settled her on the loveseat beside him.

Gus stepped forward and put out his hand. "Congratulations. You've got yourself quite a woman," he said, smiling at both of them. "The medical examiner has taken the body away and we're finished out in the stables." Gus told them both. "There's no question about the doctor being an intruder and you acting in self-defense," he said to Gillian. "There will likely be an inquest, but I'm confident in assuring you this will just be a technicality. I've got to be heading in now, but I wanted to set your mind at rest."

"Thanks Gus." Kelly stood and walked with his friend out to the gate. "You'll let me know if there's anything else you need from me, right?"

"Sure, like I said, the inquest is only a technicality. The doctor must have taken off out of that house when you and Cam moved around back. After you left we tossed a couple of smoke bombs inside and when nobody came out we figured our bird had flown. The SWAT boys went through the place, just to make sure, but he was gone all right. Like as not he came here looking for that folder you found in Sam's locker. He must have had a vehicle stashed somewhere away from the house, just in case we got him pinned down. Not that it matters now, but I'm sure glad that gal of yours has both a good head and sharp aim. You've got yourself a winner in that one.

"Thanks Gus, I appreciate the way you're handling this."

Not a problem. It's a clear case of self-defense, anybody can see that. We'd already put out a bulletin on the doctor as an armed and dangerous fugitive. I'm just glad the outcome was what it was. It could just as easily have been your lady's body in there on the floor.

"Don't remind me.. Knowing how close I came to losing her is what gave me the kick in the ass to pop the question before it was too late."

"Smart move. You've got yourself a winner." Gus slapped Kelly on the back before striding off to join the other official cars leaving the scene.

Epilogue

The inquest was over and life had finally returned to normal at the stables. The loss of Larry and Toby had left the other workers with a sense of protectiveness towards each other. Whereas before they'd always gone their separate ways when work was done, now more often than not, when the day was finished they headed out in pairs and groups for a local burger or pizza joint.

Kelly and Gillian, sitting on the back porch, on a Saturday afternoon, waved at Angelina as she hurried out of the office and down the steps to join Robin and Kevin as they came out of the gate from the stables.

"Have fun tonight," Gillian called. "They're all meeting up for to Shakespeare in the Park." She looked at Kelly brightly, and he smiled at the big grin on her face.

"Things are so much better now," she said. "I hate what happened, but I'm grateful for the way my staff has turned towards each other instead of against."

"They've got a good leader showing them the way." Kelly stood up from the swing and reached out his hand for Gillian. "I guess we'd better get out to Indian Creek before Cam sends that red head after us."

"Oh no, not that." Gillian cringed in mock horror and jumped to her feet.

"What do you think they're going to say when they get a look at this?" She lifted her hand to the sun and a rainbow of light flashed from the huge square cut diamond glittering on her finger.

Kelly covered his ears and laughed. "I can hear them now. Especially Stella."

Gillian smiled. "Wait until we tell them that we plan to have the ceremony here at Lake Country and the reception out at the Hideaway. Are you sure Cam won't mind?"

"Mind, are you kidding. That boy's going to be so damn happy it'll be all I can do to keep him from inviting everyone in the state, including the governor, who by the way, happens to be an old family friend of the Belschers."

"Oh good lord. And I was hoping for an intimate little gathering followed by a relatively small barbecue and dance."

Joining hands, they strolled out to the gate where Jake waited patiently to join them.

"You know where we're going, don't you boy?" Kelly rubbed the dog's head and opened the door of the cab so he could settle into his spot between the happy couple.

~The End~

I hope you are enjoying the Kelly McWinter P.I series. The following excerpts from the other two books in the series are for your enjoyment. *Thanks for being a reader, Jude Pittman*

Excerpt from
Deadly Secrets
Kelly McWinter PI – Book 1

Kelly stretched out in his recliner and dozed. At one-thirty, when the alarm buzzed for his two o'clock rounds at the flea market, he awoke to find that a storm had rolled in while he slept.

Kelly swiped the steaming window and squinted at the steady stream of rain that poured off the eaves. "Looks like a real gully washer." He told the dog.

Jake, who hated storms, paced anxiously back and forth from the front door to the kitchen.

"You might as well settle down. We aren't going out in that stuff. Kelly picked up the coffee pot and flicked the switch for brew then pulled a chair up to the kitchen table. When the coffee finished, he poured a cup and watched as a faint glimmer of light broke through the clouds. Giant maples thick with darkening leaves leaned across the path to the flea market. But by two o'clock the winds had receded. "Looks like it's about blown itself out." Kelly told Jake. He pulled on his boots and then grabbed a slicker out of the closet.

Jake raced across the room and stood expectantly in front of the door.

"Okay, I get it," Kelly chuckled. "Let's get on down there and get it over with."

Inside the barn that housed the flea market, the beam from Kelly's flashlight danced over sheet-covered tables. These tables were for the short-term vendors who rented from Friday to Sunday and covered their goods with sheets when they left for the night.

Permanent dealers had their own shops—enclosed three-sided cubicles with curtained entrances—where they sold everything from cultural standbys like hats, boots, jeans and t-shirts to gaudy jewelry and swirling salsa dresses. Then there were the new and used shops, like Anna's, where treasure hunters could browse through boxes of ornamental plates, old glasses and beer steins and baskets overflowing with everything from spoon collections to buttons and badges dating back to the civil war.

Kelly and Jake walked along the aisles. Gusts of wind whipped across the shrouded tables buffeting the sheets into dancing ghosts. The barn steamed with moisture left by the storm and Kelly itched to complete his rounds. He had an edgy feeling that made him anxious to get out of the barn. Jake seemed to feel it too. He paced the concrete, ears perked and alert, as if listening for something half expected.

When they finally turned into the last aisle, Kelly breathed a sigh of relief and quickened his pace. The refreshment stand, dimly lit by a Budweiser neon guitar cut in the shape of the state of Texas, loomed ahead in the shadows.

Jake had trotted ahead and he now stopped and lifted his nose, then he pulled back his lips and let out a menacing growl. Startled, Kelly clicked the flashlight on high and shone it into the refreshment stand. Inside, an old refrigerator leaned against the wall and a silver coffee urn glinted on the counter.

Kelly moved the light across the stand and shone it on the ground in front of the door. The light picked out a dark bundle that looked like rags. Kelly focused the light and started forward, moving fast. He reached a spot where the light sharpened the shadows into images, the bundle became a body and a sharp odor—the kind you never forgot—stung his nostrils.

"My God," he cried out and sprinted the distance to the booth with Jake hard on his heels.

Kelly had recognized the old, black poncho and instinct told him what to expect. Dropping to his knees, he reached out and pulled back the poncho. Jake stiffened and growled.

Anna Davis' pupils had rolled back under swollen lids and her blood-gorged tongue filled her mouth. Fighting waves of nausea, Kelly gulped air and clenched his hands into fists. After a couple minutes, he pulled himself together and got to his feet.

"Let's go boy." He cleared his throat with a kind of strangled cough. "We've got some calls to make."

Jake fell into step and they crossed to the box in front of the refreshment stand where Kelly flipped the master switch. Bright light flooded the barn and spilled across Anna. Jake growled and Kelly stroked his head. "Easy now." He settled his hand on Jake's back. "I need to call the county." Kelly pulled the phone out of his pocket and dialed the Tarrant County Sheriff's Department.

Seconds later, a crisp efficient voice said hello. Kelly identified himself, and the voice requested a report. Kelly complied. "My cabin's up at the entrance," he said, when asked to keep himself available. "I'll open the gates and wait out front for their arrival". That settled, Kelly pocketed his phone and turned to Jake. "Come on boy, let's get up the hill."

At thirty-eight Kelly still had the smooth, well-paced gait of an athlete and only a practiced eye would notice the stiffness in his left leg—a souvenir from a stray bullet.

The clouds had been swirled away by the storm's wind and now moonlight bathed the cabin in an eerie gray and orange glow that seemed to fit the night. As promised, Kelly opened the main gates, and then he and Jake headed for the cabin. On the porch he settled into an old rocker and Jake flopped at his feet. Silence, like a blanket, covered the flea market. Even the crickets were still. Mechanically, Kelly set the chair to rocking. Pictures of Anna flashed through his mind—a kaleidoscope of memories tracing the years he'd spent at Indian Creek.

Time passed and in the distance a siren sounded. Squinting northward, Kelly spotted flashes of red and blue lights. Minutes later, a patrol car turned into the yard and pulled up to the cabin.

A young deputy jumped from the car and strode to the porch. "Are you Kelly McWinter?" He was just a kid with short blonde hair trimmed close to his ears and wearing an immaculate brown-and-tan uniform. "I'm

Deputy Johnson," he said without waiting for an answer. "I understand you've got a body here."

"That's right." Kelly rose and crossed the porch to meet the officer. "She's down by the refreshment stand. I checked to make sure she was dead."

Johnson narrowed his eyes. His right hand, which had been resting comfortably on the butt of his holstered gun, stiffened.

"Nobody ever tell you not to touch a corpse?"

Kelly smiled, remembering the first time he'd been called out on a homicide. "Hey, it's all right." He kept his voice low and friendly. "I used to be on the force myself. I know the drill."

Johnson relaxed a bit but kept his hand on the holster. "Okay, just so's you didn't contaminate anything."

A squeal of tires announced the county ambulance. Two men in white overalls jumped out. A veteran with stooped shoulders and a mop of thick gray hair climbed into the back of the van and handed a large black case to a well-muscled, young Mexican.

Johnson walked over to the van, said a few words then signaled Kelly to lead the way down the hill.

Taking them through the double doors, Kelly approached the refreshment stand. "Over there." He pointed.

The younger medic stepped into the circle of light that beamed from the ceiling, set his case beside Anna's feet and started unpacking.

"Watch what the hell you're doing." The harsh voice boomed through the silent barn startling the young medic and causing him to stumble into Anna's cash box sending it skidding across the cement.

In the wake of the voice, a stocky cop with short legs and long arms stomped onto the scene. "Can't you see this is a friggin' crime scene?" The cop's thick, bulbous nose quivered and his cheeks puffed out as he let loose on the young medic. The red-faced medic bent to retrieve his case and the cop turned to Kelly.

"I'm Sergeant Adams," he said. "You the guy that reported this?"

"That's right. I'm the security guard here. I found her when I made my two o'clock rounds."

"Okay, I'll get to you in a minute."

Adams was a hard ass but Kelly sympathized. If there was any chance Anna was still alive, the medics would have priority at the scene. However, plenty of vital evidence could be destroyed in the first few minutes of an investigation. It was a standing joke with cops that an over-anxious medic was the defense attorney's best friend. They'd been known to smear fingerprints, brush off hair and fibers and wipe away any sign of bodily fluids.

Kelly had seen it all and a vivid memory of one of his own cases where an over-anxious medic had started CPR on a cold corpse popped readily to mind.

Adams and Johnson stood over the body, talking in low voices. Kelly watched as Adams bent down, lifted the poncho then dropped it back in place.

"Only an idiot would think there was any life left in that," he snapped and turned back to Johnson.

"Go call the CID, then wait out front to show the lab boys where to bring their stuff."

Done with that, he turned to the medics. "You might as well get your shit out of here," he growled. "You can stick around out front until the coroner arrives, then shove off."

The senior medic, an old-timer who looked like he'd been through this before, shrugged and motioned to his partner to step away from the body. Johnson pulled his cell out of his pocket and pressed a button. His call would bring the criminal investigations division, a team of forensic experts and the county coroner.

Kelly walked over to where Adams stood frowning at Anna's body.

"Suppose you tell me what you know about this," he growled at Kelly. "Let's sit down over there." He turned and marched over to one of the picnic tables. Kelly rolled his eyes and followed him. Adams slid onto one of the benches and Kelly eased his long frame onto the other one.

Adams took out a notebook.

Kelly propped his arm on the table and turned his mind back to the start of his rounds. Jake, who'd stood back from the group of strangers, padded over, sank down and rested his nose on Kelly's boot.

"I was doing last rounds," Kelly said. "That'd make it about two o'clock when Jake here raised his hackles and started growling."

Jake, hearing his name, lifted his eyes to the sergeant.

"You don't know Jake." Kelly reached down and stroked the dog's head. "He doesn't make a fuss without a reason, so I was edgy. There's not much goes on around here after the barn's closed up but sometimes we get kids messing around. This wasn't like that though. Jake knows the difference between kids and trouble and something was damn sure setting him off."

"Whereabouts were you when this happened?"

"About half way down that aisle." Kelly pointed toward the last row of tables. "At first I couldn't see anything but when I trained my flashlight on the refreshment stand, I spotted what looked like a bundle of rags dropped in the aisle. I clicked the beam on high and that's when I recognized Anna's poncho."

"Did you hear anything?"

"Nope, not a sound, except Jake here. He was riled something fierce."

"Okay, then what?"

"Well, like I said, I recognized that old, black poncho of Anna's. She wore it all the time. So I took off down the aisle like a bat out of hell. The poncho was wrapped around her face and I pulled it off. That was tough." Kelly squeezed his eyes shut for a moment. Then he continued. "There was a red scarf sunk so deep in her neck, I thought she'd been slashed."

"Did you touch the scarf?"

"Just the edge. I pulled her skin back a bit, to make sure but there wasn't a chance." Kelly shook his head and shuddered. "After that, I headed for the phone, got the county dispatcher and gave her the details, then Jake and I went to the cabin to wait for your deputy."

"You got any ideas who did this?"

Kelly shook his head. "Just the obvious one that comes to mind from seeing her cash box broken open and coins scattered around the ground." Kelly leaned across the table and fixed his eyes on Adams' face. "It don't make a lot of sense, y'know? If all he wanted was money, why kill her? For that matter, what was she doing prowling around down here at that time of night?"

"He?" Adams questioned.

"He...her...whatever. I guess strangling's kind of fixed in my mind as something a man would do."

"Do you know of anybody who might've had it in for Ms. Davis?"

"Hell, no. Anna was kind of an eccentric. She drank like a fish, ate like a bird and God only knows how old she was. I liked her a lot but she was a bit of a tartar—especially when she'd been hitting the bottle. Still, I can't see any of the Indian Creek folks having it in for her. They pretty much took Anna in their stride."

"We'll be wanting a list of her friends and associates from you. Deputy Johnson will attend to that. In the meantime, it'd help if you could think of someone who might know about anything out of the ordinary happening around here."

"Well, these folks are pretty closed-mouthed with strangers but you might talk to Frank Perkins — you'll find him either up at the Hideaway or down at the bait house. If anybody so much as farts on the creek, Frank knows all the details."

Adams looked up from his notebook and nodded. "We'll talk to him. What about strangers? Was there anybody who paid particular attention to Anna or asked a lot of questions about her?"

"Anna had a bit of a ruckus with one of the shoppers over at her stall this afternoon."

Adams lifted his head and fixed his eyes on Kelly. "Suppose you tell me about it."

"There was a young woman showed up here about four o'clock. She was a real looker." Kelly gave Adams a teasing grin but the officer kept his eyes on his notepad. Kelly shrugged and continued. "For some reason, this woman rushed into Anna's shop and flung herself right on top of Anna's chair. I don't know whether it was deliberate or not. All I know is when I got there, both Anna and the woman were tangled up on the floor and the woman was out cold."

"Did you recognize her?"

"Nope. She wasn't from around here—not the flea market type. I figured she might've been an antique collector. Anna had a lot of collectibles in her stall."

"Can you give me a description?"

Kelly nodded. "She was around twenty-five, about five-six, around a hundred and ten pounds I'd say with plenty of curves in all the right places. Her hair was something long and silky and so blonde it was almost white. She wore it straight down her back, held in place with one of those silk scarves."

Adams scribbled in his book. Finished, he looked up and nodded. "Go ahead."

"I spotted her soon after she came through the front entrance. She was a knockout—that's what drew my eye—but then I noticed the way she acted. It was kind of funny."

"What do you mean by funny? Did you get the impression she might be intoxicated?"

"No, nothing like that. It was more like she was trying to hide from somebody. She kept looking back over her shoulder and when she realized I had my eye on her, she scooted into the crowd like a flushed quail. Her whole manner was suspicious. That's why I followed her down to Anna's."

"Did you happen to notice if anybody was paying any special attention to this woman? Is it possible she was being followed?"

"Nope. Nobody paid her any more attention than what she'd normally get, given her looks and figure."

Adams jotted a few more lines in the book then twirled his pen again.

Kelly grinned.

"The woman?" Adams nudged.

"I was keeping my eye on her but I wasn't making it obvious. When she got next to the refreshment stand, she stopped for a bit and stood there looking kind of nervous. She'd pulled the scarf out of her hair and was kneading it with her fingers."

"What color was that scarf?"

Kelly nodded. "I know where you're going with that," he said. "It was red and yes, it could've been the one that's wrapped around Anna's neck. I'd have a hard time swearing to it though. I didn't give it more than a casual glance at the time."

Kelly paused and Adams tapped his pen on the table. "What happened next?"

"Not much. I got there right after she and Anna went down. The fall knocked her out and after I got Anna back in her chair, I turned my attention to the young woman. She'd gotten to her feet by then."

"Did you get her name?"

Kelly shook his head. "She took off before I had a chance."

"You let her go without asking any questions?"

"I wasn't thinking about questions at that point. I needed to check Anna out and make sure she was okay. Besides, she hadn't done anything except fall into a chair."

"What did Anna have to say?"

"Not a damn thing. I picked her up, brushed off her dress and asked her what happened. She wouldn't say a word, just looked up at me with those big brown eyes of hers, set her teeth on her lip and tuned me out."

"Did you get the impression Ms. Davis knew the young woman?"

"I don't know. There was something going on between them but as to whether it was recognition or just plain shock, I couldn't say." Kelly stood up and shook down his pant legs. "That's all I can tell you. I'd never seen the woman before and I don't expect you'll find anybody around here who had. Now, if you're through with me I'd like to get back to my cabin. I need to call the owner and let him know what's been going on."

Adams closed his notebook. "Okay, go ahead but keep yourself available."

Kelly nodded, signaled Jake and they headed up the hill.

Kelly's first priority was a pot of coffee. That done, he picked up the phone and dialed Shorty.

"I've got one hell of a mess out here," he said when Shorty's voice came on the line.

"Wad'ya mean, mess?"

"Someone's murdered Anna."

"Murdered. What're you talking about? I thought you were supposed to be down at the barn making rounds?"

"Where the hell do you think I've been? I found Anna's body in there about two hours ago. Some son of a bitch had taken a scarf and damn near squeezed her head off."

Kelly's hands tightened on the phone. The events of the night had taken their toll. He moved the receiver away from his mouth took a deep breath, flexed his shoulders then put the phone back to his ear. "Sorry, Shorty. I guess I'm stretched too tight."

The anger in Shorty's voice had been replaced with concern. "Not a problem, Kelly. Sounds like you've had one hell of a night. Do you want me to come over and give you a hand?"

"No. There's nothing you can do now. The place is crawling with cops. I've already told them everything I know. I'll just grab a coffee and wait until they've finished up down below."

"You'll make sure they lock up once they get done in there?"

"Don't worry about that. They'll seal the place up tight. I'll make sure though."

Hanging up the phone, Kelly eased out of his chair and stretched. His hands grazed the ceiling and he flexed his fingers against the tile.

"It doesn't look like we'll get much sleep tonight," he muttered to Jake. "Guess we might as well make ourselves comfortable while those boys take care of business."

Excerpt from

Deadly Betrayal
Kelly McWinter PI – Book 2

Mikki slipped the peach chiffon over her head, smoothed it down her hips and peered into the full-length mirror. A frown tugged at her lips and her eyes focused on the bulge below her waist.

"Darn," she muttered. "It shows already."

Tonight, over a romantic dinner, she planned to tell Alex about the baby and she didn't want him guessing beforehand.

Not long now. She glanced at her watch. In the bathroom, she applied makeup and took a brush to her short curly hair—finishing it off with a few tendrils pulled around her face. After fastening a gold chain around her neck, she slipped her feet into high-heeled sandals and stood back to inspect herself. Satisfied, she turned out the vanity light and hurried into the living room. She'd made reservations at Mystique Taverna for nine and it was nearly eight but Alex still hadn't arrived.

"I should've made them for ten," she muttered, pulling aside the draperies and peering out at the street.

Another half-hour passed before Alex's Mercedes pulled up to the curb and intending to meet him out front, Mikki grabbed her wrap, flipped off the lights and stepped into the hall. The elevator light was already lit—probably Alex—so she locked her apartment and waited.

"I'm ready," she said, when the elevator doors slid open and Alex emerged. "We've got to hurry because I made the reservations for nine."

Alex bent down and brushed her mouth with his lips.

"Sorry I'm late," he said, pulling her against his chest. "I like the dress." His hand moved over her shoulder and he slid a finger into the hollow between her breasts, pushing the chiffon aside to expose her lacy bra.

Mikki's eyes tilted to meet his. "We're going to be late," she said.

"Hmmm." He pulled her closer and slipped her bra strap down her arm. "I just want a taste," he murmured, grasping the lace with his lips and running his tongue across her nipple.

"The reservations," she moaned.

Laughing, he lifted her into his arms and swung her around to face the apartment. "We'll call them. It's not food I'm hungry for right now."

Mikki wrapped her arms around his neck and sighed. There was no use arguing with Alex.

"Hand me the key," he mumbled against her neck.

Mikki pulled it from her bag, handed it over and lay back in his arms while he unlocked the door and carried her inside.

"Let me telephone first," she begged when he started toward the bedroom. Alex chuckled, changed direction and stopped in front of the couch, where he held her suspended for a moment, then dropped her onto the soft cushions.

Mikki tossed her head in an exasperated shake and reached for the phone to call the Mystique Taverna. Alex crouched beside her and slid her dress up her legs.

Mikki bit her lip and tried to concentrate on the ringing phone while Alex's fingers explored the lace of her panties.

"Alex!" she squealed. "Don't you dare ruin them."

His eyes lit up and giving the lace a quick jerk, he pulled them free. Mikki opened her mouth to protest when a calm impersonal voice came over the wire.

"Mystique Taverna. How may I help you?"

"Oh!" She clenched her teeth and tore her thoughts away from Alex's fingers. "We have a reservation for nine and we're running late." She gasped, fighting to control her voice as Alex bent his head and touched his tongue to her belly.

"What name was that?"

"It's for Alex Wyatt," she said, stifling a moan.

"Oh, yes! We have you down."

"Could you change it to ten?"

"Of course. We'll see you then."

Alex unzipped his pants and dropped them on the floor then he lifted Mikki, slid himself onto the couch and brought her down, straddling her legs over his own.

"My dress," Mikki protested.

Alex smiled and reached for the zipper. After he'd pulled the dress over her head and tossed it aside, he grasped a nipple between his teeth and teased it into a hard nub. Mikki moaned and Alex lifted her higher sliding his tongue over the smooth skin of her belly. Digging her fingers into his shoulders, she pushed down, until she straddled his hardness. Alex grasped her buttocks and drove himself into her core.

A sliver of pain forced a small cry from Mikki's lips. Alex gripped her tighter, pulling her into his rhythm and she forgot everything—even the baby. Later, their passion spent, they collapsed against the cushions and, as usual, Alex turned away and closed his eyes.

Mikki lay with her head against his chest listening to his heartbeat. At first, it raced and fluttered, then he drifted off to sleep and it settled into a slow, monotonous rhythm. She wanted to lie there in the afterglow of their lovemaking and tell him about the baby but Alex had told her right from the start he wanted sleep, not talk, after sex. As usual, Mikki deferred to his wishes.

Sliding quietly off the couch, Mikki picked up her dress and undergarments and padded into the bedroom. After a quick shower, she lay down on the bed and had just drifted off when the telephone startled her awake. Grabbing the receiver quickly so the ringing wouldn't wake Alex, she whispered into the mouthpiece, "Hello!"

"Mikki, sweetheart. I haven't heard from you in ages." The caller's husky drawl brought a smile to Mikki's lips.

"Hi, Aunt Stella," she said. "I've been meaning to call you but it's been crazy around here. I just finished filming a video and tonight's the first night I've had free in a month."

"You've been working too hard," Stella scolded. "Why don't you come to Houston and spend some time with me?"

"Oh, Aunt Stella, I'd love to but I have a complication in my life right now that's going to require most of my attention for the next seven months."

"You're not?" Stella gave a delighted shout. "You rascal, you. I'd given up hope of ever being a Great-Auntie Stella."

Mikki laughed. At thirty-eight, Stella was more like an elder sister than an aunt. It hadn't taken her a minute to figure out what the seven months implied and she wasn't the least bit shocked.

"I wish your reaction was what I could expect from the rest of my family," Mikki said.

"Pooh on them. They're a bunch of old fogies. You let me take care of the family. Now tell me. When is your due date and what are your plans? Why don't you come stay with me?"

"Let me catch my breath," Mikki said, laughing at Stella's exuberance. "I don't know what I'm going to do yet. I haven't told the father and it's just possible he might have some ideas along those lines."

"Oh, men! What do they know about having babies? Okay, I won't push you but give it some thought. I'm going nuts rattling around in this ten-room house by myself. I'd love to have you stay with me until the baby comes—and for as long after as you want. I'm sure you know you're always welcome."

"Thank you!" Mikki's voice caught in her throat. "You're wonderful, Aunt Stella and I promise, I'll call you just as soon as I've had a chance to talk to Alex."

"Alex Wyatt!" Stella snapped the name.

"I know you don't like him." Mikki swallowed to keep the hurt out of her voice. "But I love him so much and I know he's going to make a wonderful father."

"I'm sorry, sweetie." Stella hurriedly retracted the angry words she'd spoken at the mention of Alex's name. "I didn't mean to snarl. I don't care who the father is as long as he takes care of you. When are you planning to tell him?"

"Tonight. We're going out for dinner. I'll tell him then." "Well, good luck, kid and call me later, will you?"

"I will, Aunt Stella. And thanks."

* * *

Stella hung up the telephone and grabbed a pillow off of the sofa. "Damn," she cursed, punching her fist into the pillow. "That son of a bitch is going to break her heart."

Clamping a cigarette between her lips, she pulled open the top drawer of her desk and grabbed a thick address book. Opening the book, she flipped rapidly through the pages to the name McWinter.

Marking the spot with a finger, she reached for the phone and with a sharp red fingernail, tapped out the number.

Kelly McWinter was the Fort Worth detective who'd been instrumental in catching the murderer of Stella's husband and sister-in-law the previous year. He had become a friend during the long months of the investigation. He'd promised to be there if Stella ever needed his help and right now seemed like a good time to test the promise.

"Be there," Stella muttered as she counted the rings. "Hello!" Kelly's soft drawl sent a tingle down her spine. "Kelly! Thank God! I was afraid you'd be away on a job."

"Hi, Stella!" Kelly's voice warmed with recognition. "Must be that ESP of yours," he said. "I just got back from Beaumont this morning."

"I need you to check someone out for me." "You've only got to ask."

"It's my niece, Mikki. She's gotten herself pregnant by a jerk named Alex Wyatt. He's married and I've heard a few rumors about him that have me worried. Maybe you've heard of his wife? She's the former Lorena Miller, daughter of one of those Texas oil millionaires."

"Can't say as I have but then I don't exactly move in those circles."

"Smart man," Stella mumbled. "Alex and Lorena are supposed to be big news with the Dallas social set and I thought maybe you could do some checking on him. Alex will probably give Mikki the brush-off as soon as he finds out about the baby but I'd like to know a bit more about him just in case."

"Consider it done," Kelly said. "I'll get hold of Jim Forbes. He's a friend of mine on the Dallas PD. If there's any dirt on Wyatt, Jim will dig it out."

"Thanks, Kelly. I knew I could count on you."

"No problem. I'll try to get hold of him tonight. Now, before I let you off the line, I have a favor to ask. I've been talking to the recruiter at American Mutual Indemnity in Sugar Land. They need another investigator on their staff and I have an appointment on Monday. I thought it might be fun to combine business with the pleasure of your company—that is, if you can put me up for a couple of days?"

"Can I? You know damn well I can. Besides, having you around will take my mind off Mikki's troubles. And don't forget to bring that mutt Jake along."

"Good! I'll have a talk with Jim tonight and, depending on how fast he can dig up the information on Wyatt, I'll see you either late tomorrow afternoon or early evening."

"Wonderful! I'll be waiting."

* * *

After her talk with Stella, Mikki hung up the phone and lay back down on the bed. Stella's reserve about Alex had intensified her own fears but she absolutely refused to believe he wouldn't be happy about their baby. Months ago he'd told her Lorena refused to get pregnant because it might spoil her figure and there'd been real bitterness in his voice. Mikki was sure he'd go ahead with a divorce once he heard the news.

From the living room came sounds of Alex moving around. Slipping into her dress, Mikki smoothed her hair one last time and hurried to meet him.

In the car, Alex drove with one hand on the wheel and the other stroking her thigh. "I see you've climbed a couple more notches up the charts," he said.

Mikki nodded. "Mike's thinking about having me do a single but I don't know if I'm ready right now. I may take a few months off."

"Better not." He shook his head. "The public's fickle and you need to strike while the group's hot. If I were you, I'd listen to Mike. He's the best there is. That's why I've got him working for Miller-Wyatt."

Mikki kept her thoughts to herself. She was sure Alex would change his mind once he knew she was pregnant. He wouldn't want her endangering the baby by going through those long, grueling recording sessions.

The car lurched and swerved. "Shit," Alex snapped and jerked the wheel. "I think I've got a flat."

"Oh, no! It's twenty to ten. What will the people at Mystique think if I have to call them again?"

"Screw Mystique. It'll probably take an hour for the auto club to get here this time of night. I'll have to change the damn thing myself."

He got out of the car and bent down to look at the tire. "It's flat all right," he muttered, reaching inside to pull the keys. "You better get out while I jack it up."

Alex opened the trunk and took out the tire bar and lug wrench. "Hold onto these while I get this tire out of here," he said, handing her the tools and bending over to grab the spare. Mikki followed him to the front of the car and dutifully handed him the tire bar.

"I feel like a nurse," she giggled.

Alex grunted and bent to the job of removing the lugs and pulling off the old tire. After he had the new tire in place, he tightened the lug nuts and handed her the wrench. "Put those back in the trunk," he snapped.

Mikki replaced them and grabbed a rag from the box. "Here, you can wipe your hands," she said when he'd finished storing the tire.

He grunted and grabbed the rag. "What time is it?" he asked.

"Ten minutes to ten. That didn't take long. We should get there right on time." "Hell of a way to start the night," he muttered.

Mikki climbed into the car and shut her eyes. She'd wanted tonight to be so perfect but the flat tire had put a damper on things. Alex's good mood had evaporated and a headache had started pounding away at her temples.

* * *

They rode the rest of the way in silence. Mikki kept her eyes closed until Alex swerved into Mystique's driveway and stopped the car. The Taverna, a long low building set discreetly back from the street, had been painted a deep Mediterranean blue, its entrance flanked by two Romanesque columns. Mystique had been etched into the black woodwork and a brass ring hung from the set of double doors.

After turning the car over to a valet, Alex grasped Mikki's elbow and guided her up the short flight of stone steps.

"Ready?" He smiled down at her.

She nodded and Alex pulled the ring. The doors swung open, admitting them into a cool, dim foyer with frescoed walls and plush green carpeting.

"Good evening, Mr. Wyatt." A smiling maître d' stepped forward. "You're looking charming this evening, Miss Benson."

"Thank you," Mikki acknowledged the compliment.

Alex kept his hand pressed against her waist as they crossed the room to an intimate table set up on one of the small platforms surrounding the main dining area.

Mikki and Alex smiled and nodded to mutual acquaintances as they crossed the room. At the table, a waiter appeared with a menu. "Mr. Marston has ordered a bottle of Andre Brunel Cotes Du Rhone for you and Miss Benson," he said, motioning toward a thin, gray-haired man with wire-rimmed spectacles and a beak nose, who was cuddled up to an attractive brunette at the opposite side of the platform.

Alex turned and waved a thank you. "We'll start with a gin martini and a daiquiri," he said. "I'll give you our order later."

Handing back the menu, Alex turned to Mikki. "Is that okay with you?" he asked. Mikki hesitated, then said to the waiter, "I'd like that daiquiri virgin, please."

He nodded and went to fill their order.

Alex leaned his elbows on the crisp white cloth, reached for the centerpiece — a cornucopia of fresh fruit and crimson dahlias—and shoved it aside. "You're not going to be a drag are you?" His eyes gripped hers.

"I've got a bit of a headache." She flushed uncomfortably. "I'll feel better after I have something to eat."

Alex nodded. "I'll go have a word with Kenneth," he said, rising to leave the table.

Mikki smiled wearily. She frequently spent half the night sitting alone while Alex table-hopped. Watching him cross the floor, she felt a tightness in her chest. He was so good-looking—tall and slender with thick, blond hair and piercing blue eyes set off by a deeply tanned face.

A lot of women yearned to be in Mikki's shoes and as she watched Alex cross to the table occupied by Winn and Theresa Gordon, the memory of a rumor she'd heard sprung to mind. Winn was a sales representative for Wyatt Recording and Alex had spent a weekend at the Gordons' ranch a couple months ago. One of the rumors circulating at Wyatt Recording was that Winn had been out of town the weekend Alex paid his visit.

Watching him greet the Gordons, Mikki wondered about Winn—a colorless, nondescript, little man who paled beside Theresa — a cool, elegant brunette with hungry eyes. Rumor had it she'd slept with half the men at Wyatt Recording. Mikki had put the rumors down to jealous gossip but now, watching Theresa plaster herself against Alex, she wondered.

Turning away, Mikki's mind wandered back to her first date with Alex. She'd grown up in the small town of Maryville, Tennessee and after winning a talent contest sponsored by a local radio station, she'd received an invitation to audition with the Livewires, a hot new country rock band from Nashville. They'd loved her voice and hired her on the spot. Her father had ranted when she told him but Mikki had refused to give up the job. Leaving her mother to deal with her dad's anger, she'd moved to Nashville. Mikki had met Alex, the Dallas-based owner of Wyatt Recording when he'd stopped by the studio to watch a recording session and when he invited her out to dinner, she'd awkwardly accepted.

For their first date, he'd picked her up in a limousine and taken her on the General Jackson. It had been Mikki's first time on a riverboat and she'd been thrilled. Alex had told her he was married but that he and his wife lived separate lives. She'd had some qualms but Alex had been a perfect gentleman and they'd had a wonderful time. After the date, he'd sent her two dozen, long-stemmed red roses and the deliveries had continued all week.

The following Saturday, when he called for another date, Mikki had laughingly told him that if he didn't stop the deliveries, she was going to have to move or open a flower shop.

"You seem deep in thought," Alex said, returning to the table.

Mikki smiled up at him. "I was thinking about our first date and all those roses you sent me."

Alex grinned. He liked being the center of her thoughts.

"Are you ready to order, sir?" The waiter appeared at Alex's elbow.

"I think so. We'll start with a spanakopita, then Greek salad and the arni psito, I think."

"Very good." The waiter noted the order in his little book. "Would you care for the wine now?" he asked. "Or do you wish another cocktail?"

"The wine," Alex replied.

The waiter hurried off and Alex turned back to Mikki. "Okay," he said. "You've got something on your mind. I can tell by the way you've been moping. Let's get it over with, shall we? Then maybe we can enjoy our dinner."

Mikki's face dropped. She hadn't realized her anxiety was so obvious. "I'm going to have a baby." She surprised herself by blurting it out.

Alex stared. His hand reached for his glass and he drained the rest of his drink. "When?"

Mikki laughed. "Not for another seven months."

"Good!" He set his glass back on the table. "You'll have plenty of time to get an abortion. I'll find you a good doctor."

Mikki recoiled as if she'd been slapped. Her face blanched and tears rushed to her eyes.

"What's the matter?" Alex's eyes searched her face. "Are you going to be sick?" Mikki shook her head. She couldn't speak.

"You're not going to be stupid about this, are you?" he growled. "Surely you know a baby is out of the question." Alex seemed genuinely confused. "Damn!" He dug in his pocket for his cigar case.

"I will not kill my baby." Hysteria rose in Mikki's throat. She fought it down and forced herself to meet his eyes.

Alex shook his head. "Fuck!" He slammed his case down on the table.

Mikki stood up and clutched her stomach, as if to shield the baby. "I'm going to have this baby and nothing you say or do is going to stop me."

A hush fell over the dining room and several heads turned toward their table but Mikki kept her eyes fixed on Alex. Tears streamed down her face. "I never want to see you again," she choked, grabbing her bag and starting down the steps.

"Wait a minute." Alex jumped up and reached for her arm.

Mikki jerked away from him, eyes blazing. "If you so much as touch me, I'll kill you," she shrieked.

An elderly woman, passing their table, gasped and clamped her hand to her mouth. Ignoring the woman, Mikki whirled and raced for the lobby.

"Please call me a taxi," she sobbed to the bewildered maître d' before she raced out of the restaurant.

Note from the Publisher

Thank you for purchasing and reading this Books We Love eBook. We hope you have enjoyed your reading experience. Books We Love and the author would very much appreciate you returning to the online retailer where you purchased this book and leaving a review for the author. *Best Regards and Happy Reading, Jamie and Jude*

Books We Love Ltd.
http://bookswelove.net

Top quality books loved by readers,
Romance, Mystery, Fantasy, Young Adult
Vampires, Werewolves, Cops, Lovers.

Looking for Something Spicier
Try Books We Love Spice
http://spicewelove.com

Also published by Books We Love

Deadly Secrets
Deadly Betrayal
Bad Medicine

Made in the USA
Charleston, SC
19 October 2012